Melbourne Writers Social Group Short Stories

Authors:
Solene Anglaret
Angelique Benoit
Allan Carter
Mat Clarke
Sohom Das
Christie Heart
Ander Louis
Dean MacAllister
Adam Mitchell
Magz Morgan
Chun Kiu Ng
Elly Parkinson
Jeremy Picknell
Kerry Sharp
Katarina Smythe
Jo Stanford

First release in August 2019
Editor: **Mat Clarke**
Front cover design: **Elly Parkinson**

Produced and published by Melbourne Writers
ISBN 9780463554746

Melbourne Writers Social Group Anthology
A winter Selection of Short Stories

Table of Contents

Theme: Holidays / Special Events

1 Sand and Locusts *by Christine Heart*   Page 10
Christie Heart is an Australian author, songwriter and artist who lives in rural Victoria. Her debut novel Leave The Wake Behind (general fiction), comes with a Cd of original songs and enjoys high rotation throughout library services in Victoria. She is currently writing short stories and a reality/fantasy novel aimed at YA readers, with several general fiction novels in various stages of production
www.christieheart.com

2 The Final Straight *by Allan Carter*   Page 13
Allan Carter is a retired teacher who has an interest in writing poetry, short stories and children's pieces

3 Jason's Christmas List *by Jeremy Picknell*   Page 15
Jeremy Picknell is a composer and writer of both music theatre and fiction. He is currently finishing his first future fiction novel.
jeremypicknell@gmail.com

4 Merry Bloody Xmas *by Katarina Smythe*   Page 18
Katarina lives on the Mornington Peninsula. She publishes romance under the pen name Kaydence Snow and is an International Bestselling author.
www.kaydencesnow.com/

From an early age, Mat has used a keyboard as the instrument of his expression. His range is broad, from the chilling, to the obscure, to fan fiction, to thought provoking, to children's and YA, and a not too small amount of speculative fiction. Yet, his main area of interest has always been the thriller genre
www.worldwriterscollective.com/mat-carke

Theme: Betrayal

Dean MacAllister lives in Melbourne, Australia. He is a seasoned world traveller, scuba diver and avid lover of writing and reading fiction. He has previously published stories in multiple magazines, zines and competitions worldwide, including EWR, AWR, Jitter Press, Creepy Cabin, Untitled, Haunted MTL, is a regular in Weirdbook and his first novel 'The Misadventures of a Reluctant Traveller' is now available on Amazon. For more of his works make sure you check out www.deanmacallister.com

Passionate teacher, passionate writer. Eyes and heart open, always learning.

Allan Carter is a retired teacher who has an interest in writing poetry, short stories and children's pieces

 From an early age, Mat has used a keyboard as the instrument of his expression. His range is broad, from the chilling, to the obscure, to fan fiction, to thought provoking, to children's and YA, and a not too small amount of speculative fiction. Yet, his main area of interest has always been the thriller genre www.worldwriterscollective.com/mat-carke

10 Snog, Marry or Kill *by Elly Parkinson* Page 52
Elly is an up and coming Melbourne Author, specialising in theatre, drama and darker stories.

Theme: Heroes and Villains

11 Changing Winds *by Jo Stanford* Page 53
Writing helps me see.
I like to define and interpret experiences through words on a page. My own, or an imaginary character who's just like us. Someone who loves and hurts and seeks a path to navigate life's ordeals. When I put their (or my) story into words, it makes more sense. I can start to see a way.
Writing is my teacher.

12 Pyrrhic Victory *by Chun Kiu Ng* Page 61
As an avid reader of fantasy books growing up, Chun aspires to create worlds of his own that captures the imagination
chunkiu.ng@gmail.com
www.worldwriterscollective.com/chun-kiu-ng)

13 Live Free or Die *by Angelique Fawns* Page 71
Angelique Fawns writes speculative fiction, and loves featuring unusual protagonists.
fawns.ca/twitter.com/raingirl51

Dean MacAllister lives in Melbourne, Australia. He is a seasoned world traveller, scuba diver and avid lover of writing and reading fiction. He has previously published stories in multiple magazines, zines and competitions worldwide, including EWR, AWR, Jitter Press, Creepy Cabin, Untitled, Haunted MTL, is a regular in Weirdbook and his first novel 'The Misadventures of a Reluctant Traveller' is now available on Amazon. For more of his works make sure you check out www.deanmacallister.com

Jeremy Picknell is a composer and writer of both music theatre and fiction. He is currently finishing his first future fiction novel.
jeremypicknell@gmail.com

Theme: Stranger

Kerry enjoys all forms of writing.
www.kerrysharp.com/

Dr Das is a Consultant Forensic Psychiatrist who rehabilitates mentally ill offenders. He writes a blog about mental health issues for the Huffington Post:
www.huffingtonpost.co.uk/author/dr-sohom-das/
His other published short stories can be found on this author website:
www.sdas-author.com

Editor's Introduction

These stories you are about to read have been created under many different circumstances. I hope, therefore, each one comes across as unique and entertaining and you'll continue to think about the characters, the story and the authors, well after you finish reading.

Before each story most authors have included notes that you may find interesting. None of them give away the ending, but some do give you an idea of the thought process behind the work. If you prefer not to be informed about the "behind the scenes" creative side, feel free to skip over each one.

There are four themes for the stories which have been created through story competitions over the last one-plus years (2018). You'll also find a few different genres within these pages. Each is enjoyable in their own way.

It is the authors' hope that you enjoy all the stories and go on to tell friends of the ones you enjoyed the most. Feel free to look the authors up online and let them know your thoughts too.

Many of the authors are listed on the World Writers Collective website.

Thank you to our judges for making us better writers:

Jacqueline Cripps
www.worldwriterscollective.com/jacqueline-cripps

Christie Heart
www.worldwriterscollective.com/christie-heart

Kerry Sharp
www.worldwriterscollective.com/kerry-sharp

Dorothy Shorne
www.worldwriterscollective.com/dorothy-shorne

Suraya Dewing
www.worldwriterscollective.com/suraya-dewing

1. Sand and Locusts *by Christie Heart*

Author's note: Sand And Locusts was inspired by my experience as a housekeeper in a coastal holiday resort.

*

Kira pushed the heavily laden trolley to room 507. She knocked hard on the door three times. "Housekeeping." No reply. Another two knocks. "Housekeeping," she called again, as she opened the door.

Champagne bottles and wilting roses. She grinned. *Lovers nest.* Stripping the bed with practiced speed, a used sachet of strawberry flavoured lube confirmed her theory.

Room 515. Twin beds, sandy footprints on the carpet, sticky prints over every surface. *Children!* There was no accompanying grin.

As Kira toiled she dreamed of her own holiday. *Only three days now.* First, the Maldives. A thatched hut over white sands and aqua waters. Then a five day safari through the Kruger National Park. Wedding bells in London and honeymoon on the Greek Islands. Throughout the back-breaking summer, saving for this wedding trip with her fiancée, Ian, kept her cheerful and sane. She glanced at the indent on her left ring finger, her diamond solitaire was safer kept at home.

The locusts have landed! Room 525 was stripped of every freebie down to the last sachet of equal. *Why not? I might do the same.* For the final time Kira heaved the trolley through the laundry door, unloaded cleaning products, used rags, rubbish and recyclables. Inside the staffroom the housekeeping crew gathered with hugs and well-wishes. She collected her final payslip from the smiling manager and headed home on golden wings.

Sorry

The note lay in the centre of the vacant room. *What?* Kira rushed into the bedroom. Empty. Kitchen the same. Shock hit like a wall. Back in the lounge, she collapsed onto the carpet. Picking up the paper, she turned it over. Nothing. Just the single word. Through the numbness and disbelief a thought struck.

Shaking fingers fumbled the phone from her bag. She stabbed in the digits for internet banking and waited while it accessed the joint travel account. Balance ZERO dollars. Her personal savings? Ditto. The phone slipped from her hand.

"Nohhhhh … !" She rocked and keened. *This couldn't be happening!*

Time elapsed and as a last ditch she called the travel agent.

"Kira, how unexpected." The woman's voice was cool. "How was your flight? Have you arrived in Hong Kong?"

"Hong Kong? What do you mean? We're supposed to be flying to Male this Tuesday."

The agent sounded confused. "But you cancelled that itinerary weeks ago in exchange for an open ticket to Hong Kong. I must say I was surprised."

"Jane, I know nothing of this."

"I don't understand?"

"Ian's gone. Everything's gone ..." Kira broke down.

Jane's voice became serious. "Kira, do you have your passport?"

"No, nothing. I just got home from work. I'm still in my uniform. The house is completely stripped."

"Listen Kira. You need to call the police immediately. I think you might be the victim of identity theft."

"What?!"

"Kira, two people came in to change those travel arrangements. One was Ian. I swear the woman looked just like you."

Numbness. Kira struggled to breathe.
"Oh and Kira, she was wearing your ring."
© Christie Heart 2017

Author's note: The race for the Melbourne Cup does not always go to the swift.

*

Scaramouche felt the sand give way beneath his hooves. The mist from his nostrils mingled with the spray from the waves. The air was crisp and its coolness brushed his flanks, producing a gentle tingling which he found exhilarating. It was the last workout before the Big Day.

Back in the stables, Scaramouche found Lady Godiva leaning against him. He looked at her beautiful nose – a nose that had won her many a race. She nudged him softly.

"It's a pity we have to share these stables with those international upstarts. Look at that nag over there – Belle Poitrine. She thinks she's above the rest of us simply because some wealthy Arab has brought her here. The race should only be for good Aussie horses," Lady Godiva snorted.

"The race will sort her out," Scaramouche replied. "Her legs are not as good as yours."

Lady Godiva exposed her teeth in an expansive grin. She had enjoyed Scaramouche's company for the past two years. She did not mind that he was a gelding. His calm nature appealed to her. The stallions were rough and frisky and she often had to resist their advances.

They lived for the race-track. There was nothing like the dash down the straight, crossing the finish line ahead of every other horse. Tomorrow would be the biggest day of all – the Melbourne Cup.

Scaramouche enjoyed the special preparation. Of particular pleasure was the rubdown from the strapper, a teenage girl who whispered in his ear as she caressed him with the brush against his upper body.

In the stables that night, the horses showed different aspects of their personalities. Scaramouche thought about the riding techniques of various jockeys. Some used the whip harshly. Others used the whip sparingly whilst speaking quietly into the horse's ear. These were the ones who did not see riding as merely a job, but as a union between human and horse.

The Melbourne Cup had arrived. After the preparation, they all headed for the starting barrier and were pushed into their individual starting gates. Belle Poitrine was the last in; her petulance ensuring all attention was focussed on her.

They were off. Scaramouche was somewhere in the middle of the field. He was running freely and was moving toward the inside rail. He could feel that most of the other horses were now behind him.

Midway down the straight, Scaramouche found himself near the rails. He was blocked in. Belle Poitrine edged closer, then pushed him. He hit the rails and fell. His legs gave way and he heard the distinct crack of a bone.

Scaramouche saw movement around him. From a distance, muffled sounds came in waves upon the wind. Curtains were closed around where he lay.

There was cheering and adulation for the winning horse. People lifted glasses of champagne or clutched the tickets that would bring unexpected rewards.

No-one heard the solitary shot that brought Scaramouche to the finish line.

3 Jason's Christmas List *by Jeremy Picknell*

Author's note: When writing to a theme, I write the first thing that comes to mind and let all meaning be derived from that.

*

"Mum," cried Jason as he ran out of After School Care, arms outstretched for a hug. Once around the corner of the building, he doubled backed and waved good-bye to the staff through the window.

"Mum says Merry Christmas!"

Jason hid behind the hedge and waited. He knew the staff had sneaked a Christmas drink when they thought the kids weren't looking and along with it being the last day, he gambled that they wouldn't insist on his mum coming in to sign him out.

Once satisfied they had bought his ruse, Jason ran the kilometre home. Then, full of guilty excitement, he did the one thing he was forbidden to do; switch on the computer in her study, without her there to supervise. The clock said 5:05pm, one hour before she would turn up to After School Care, stressed and apologetic, as if it was the first time she had ever been late.

Jason Googled 'Death Hunt,' which he had overheard some bigger X-Box kids brag about. A picture of a creature, half-man, half-beast appeared with blood-stained muscular chest, carrying a massive bazooka. In the background was a cool looking scene of carnage. Jason was over the moon, not just at the picture, but that it was available on PlayStation.

A photo popped up on the side of the screen. It was, (at least what he considered), an old man, smiling with slick black hair and shirt, a bit like what he imagined his father looked like. Above it were some words about a deal, valid only until Christmas. Jason looked back at Death Hunt and carefully checked that three was the latest version.

From the desk drawer, he took out a note pad and wrote:

SANTA LIST FOR JASON
PG Game (don't care which)
Death Hunt 3 FOR PLAYSTATION (just between you and me)

He wondered what he should get for his mum. On the computer, there was a different pop up-guy this time, a blonde one with a slightly wussy tattoo. In his arms was a very happy woman. He read the advert again. Jason knew enough about the internet to know that pop-ups come up because it knows exactly what people are wanting, without them even realizing it. So, he added to his list:

A packit of Tinder Gold (to give to Mum)

Jason closed down the computer and raced back to school, beating his mother by only seconds. Before she could get out the car, he jumped in.

"Don't worry, Mum, they've gone home. They couldn't wait any longer."

"Oh," she said, confused.

Jason held up an envelope.

"Can we drop this in Santa's box in the Mall, on the way home?"

"Not now darling, I need to get dinner on," she said, smiling more to herself than him. "I'll do it tomorrow on the way to the hairdresser."

"Do you promise not to look at it?"

She ruffled his hair.

“I promise.”

4 Merry Bloody Xmas *by Katarina Smythe*

Author's note: The pressure of working in retail and dealing with her obnoxious family, make for a memorable Christmas Eve for Anna.

*

Christmas carols on a loop, rude customers, long shifts – nothing destroys one's faith in humanity like working in retail during the holidays. Instead of going home after a gruelling shift, Anna drove an hour to her Aunt Penny's house for Christmas Eve dinner.

It began to snow as Anna pushed the door of her aunt's house open, the extravagant wreath flopping against it. Her triplet cousins ploughed into her, screaming as they shoved past, not even acknowledging her presence.

"Hello to you too." She muttered to herself as she removed layers of clothing. It was stifling inside.

Anna walked into the living room where everyone was already seated at a long table. The centrepiece of the room was a massive Christmas tree. It was draped in white ornaments and glowed with lights. In an armchair next to it, her dad was fast asleep, undisturbed by the cacophony of screaming children, babbling adults, and clinking glassware.

Everyone seemed to notice her at once, yelling over the top of each other to admonish her for being late, question her life choices, make fun of her work uniform, and complain about how far away she lived. Her great uncle even managed to work in an offensive comment about 'the gays'.

Anna's left eye began to twitch. Her breaths became shallow and uneven. Her shoulders tensed as she worked hard to calm the rage inside.

Her cousin Paul chose that moment to barrel into her with

a bowl of eggnog, dumping the entire contents down her back.

"Watch it Anna!" he snapped, unapologetic. *Typical.*

Standing in a pool of sticky judgement and overwhelm, Anna snapped.

She released a guttural scream, snatching the eggnog bowl and bringing it down onto Paul's head. It made a sickening crunch, and Paul crumpled to the floor, the gash in his forehead oozing blood and mixing with the yellowish gloop of the eggnog.

Jumping over Paul's body, she launched herself at the dregs of humanity she had the privilege of calling her family.

Several moments later Anna found herself standing in the middle of the long table, surveying her work. Her relatives lay about the room dead or dying as warm blood dripped off almost every surface. Anna held the carving knife tightly at her side, blood oozing off the tip of the blade.

Breathing hard, her attention was drawn to the beautiful tree. It was the only item in the room that had escaped her rage, still glowing ethereally in the midst of the carnage.

"I'm sorry Anna." Paul apologised, pulling her back out of her dark fantasy. "I'll get you a towel."

"Thanks, Paul." The noises of playing children and half-drunk adults came back to her as she felt the eggnog soaking into the top of her underwear.

It was cathartic to imagine ending them all in a graphic way, but now the rage was draining out of Anna and she was looking forward to her aunt's famous turkey. She was starving.

"Hope you're all hungry!" The bird in question came through the door, perched on a platter held by Aunt Penny.

5 Roadside *by Mat Clarke*

Author's note:
Have you ever read *Stephen King on Writing*? Maybe this story will make you think about that one time he went for a walk along the side of the road and had an unfortunate accident.

*

Cloudy. That was Larry's first thought. Although there were blue patches too. He turned his head to the side. Stones raked the back of his head.

"Shit, ow."

His voice came out as a bark.

"Oh, crap," he laughed. "Drunk and sleeping on the side of the road. What a dickhead."

He tried rolling onto his side, but was barely able to move and felt like vomiting with the attempt.

"Fuck that," he said, feeling less mirthful with the pain.

He turned his head the other way and saw a road disappearing past a rotting fence that continued on and wrapped around the side of a green grassy hill. His surroundings appeared to be somewhat familiar, but he found it hard to grasp onto any one memory. And although that was likely due to last night's drinks, it was still disconcerting. In addition, he could now see that someone was lying right next to him and keeping just as still as him. The person's lower half was all he could see past his own fat belly. And he (deciding the person next to him was a 'he' because of his style of clothing) was wearing light blue jeans that had been torn around the knee to reveal a splattering of dried blood.

"Hey, you okay?" Larry said. "I can get you some help?"
Larry worked his hand toward his pocket and his phone.
The guy's leg moved.

"Hey, hey, you're gonna be okay. I'm trying to get help, just hold on, can you tell me your name?"

The person didn't answer. Larry kept reaching for his phone, while also raising his head to try and see more of the guy, although with little success. He regretted last night now and the many Christmas lunches he had eaten before finally attending his own works' Christmas dinner. God, he was getting big.

"Fat bastard. Okay, diet starts tomorrow." He already had his stomach set for pizza tonight, so he would start on the diet tomorrow.

"Yeah, tomorrow then."

Just as he reached the top edge of his phone in his pocket, a police car came around the bend heading toward them. Larry sighed and let out a long slow breath. Now they could help the guy lying next to him, and lend him a hand as well.

The officer got out of the car and a man in an orange hi-vis and Santa hat followed after. Their expressions showed that whatever had happened to the guy lying next to Larry, he was in serious trouble. Larry tried to look sober and professional, but guessed he appeared as dopey as he felt.

"You alright?" the officer said. "Can you talk?"

Larry listened for a reply from the unfortunate guy next to him, then decided to speak for him.

"He hasn't said anything, but he moved his leg. He's alive, I'm sure of that."

The officer turned to the man in the orange hi-vis standing a little behind him.

"Was there someone else?"

The man shook his head.

The officer turned back to Larry.

"Sir, there's no one else around. Do you know what's going on?"

Larry rolled his eyes and explained what had happened from the moment he woke until now.

The officer's face paled the more Larry spoke. The man behind the officer turned and faced the other way, his head in his hands.

The officer came closer to Larry and said, "Sir, you're alone. Two hours ago, this gentleman behind me was driving his work van from a Christmas party when he lost control and collided with you along the roadside. Right now, his van is on top of your lower body. I'm very sorry, but until the paramedics arrive I won't be able to move you."

Larry stared at the leg next to him and this time recognised his footwear.

"That's your leg up next to you, sir, everything else from your waist down is compacted underneath the metal frame of the van, there may be nothing we can do even after the ambulance arrives. The paramedics said that when the van is lifted up from you, you'll . . ." The cop took off his cap and wiped his forehead. ". . . you'll be deceased in minutes. The best idea is to leave the van where it is so you can get anyone down here that you need to see. Sir, is there anyone I can call?"

Larry stared back up at the sky, which had now fully clouded over. He was fat and he hated that it would be the last memories his wife and children would have of him before he took his final breath.

6 Not About You *by Dean MacAllister*

Author's note: Today is the day of the funeral. But today isn't about him. Today Rebecca is finally going to set the record straight.

*

The weather today was forecast to be wet and miserable, with a chance of mourning.

Rebecca put on a blouse, the third she had tried so far, while staring at herself in the mirror. She didn't own much black clothing, so if this top wasn't just right then she would have to go out and buy a new one. Straightening it out, she appraised her reflection. The top showed off a hint of a bra, with just the right amount of cleavage. Modest enough not to look slutty. Sexy enough to draw the attention she required. Perfect. She smiled. She felt calmer now.

The rant she had in the shower had been rehearsed over and over again, until she memorised every wrong that he had done her. It was therapeutic, spitting out your grievances into the echo of a steamy bathroom, the hot water washing your vitriol down the sink as you vented. Every scene seemed to replay itself off the shower screen, projecting memories of slights and arguments, disappointments and frustrations. She had scrubbed herself raw until the water had run cold.

Rebecca turned to her side, her eyes running up and down her figure. She had always been a thin girl, but she was slowly developing some curves now she had reached her thirties. Despite a couple of grey hairs, her long, straight black hair was well looked after. She had once been told that she would have been such a beautiful girl, if she could only stop frowning. She tried to walk around with a smile after being told that, but after

23

only a few hours her scowl had returned to rest on her face.

What was there in life to smile about?

What was the point of any of it?

The one thing she had wanted was out of her reach now, unobtainable more than ever before. He was gone. Gone without ever providing what she needed most. How selfish a man he was, to leave without even saying goodbye, without giving her the affirmation she had needed so badly. Life had always been about him; what he wanted, what he needed to achieve. She always had to compete to catch his eye. To get his attention. But today she would get the attention that she deserved. If they weren't willing to give it to her, then she would take it.

Sitting down at her vanity table she studied her face. Deep lines were etched across her forehead, ones that refused to disappear even when she forced a smile. It gave her a constantly serious look that made her rare laughter alarming for those who witnessed it, as if it was a howl of pain rather than that of pleasure. The few attempts she had made at online dating seemed quickly to come to an end when her laughter escaped. She tried her best to suppress it, but it would claw its way out, a sad and nervous bark, giving the impression of desperation hiding just beneath the skin.

Applying red lipstick carefully, she made a kiss-face to check that it was on properly. She gave the tiniest of smiles, the kind that you would give to a stranger in the street, or to the person packing your groceries. It was the best that she could do.

She looked at her watch. 10 am.

The service would have started by now.

Taking a deep breath, she stared at her pale reflection, trying not to hate what she saw. She sighed loudly, her exclamation ringing out in the large, empty house. Grabbing her handbag, she put on her shoes and opened the front door.

Outside the rain had died down to a light drizzle. The dark clouds gave the impression that it was early evening. She dashed for her car. The car's interior lights turned on as she approached and, sensing the keys in her pocket, unlocked itself as she grabbed the door handle. Jumping in, she lowered the visor and re-checked her makeup. Her mascara had already begun to run. Taking a small packet of tissues out of her handbag, she tried to fix it up as best she could. She pushed the ignition button on the dash and the car woke up, loudly at first, but dying down as the motor warmed up. The automatic wipers turned on and she pulled out onto the road.

There weren't many cars out on this overcast Sunday morning. Most people would have been relaxing with their families, stoking their fireplaces while watching television, getting cosy under blankets. But attending his funeral, Rebecca couldn't think of anywhere she would rather be today. Today they would shut up and listen. Today they wouldn't be able to ignore her. Today she would have her turn to speak.

She looked down at her speed and eased her foot off the accelerator. It would not do to be pulled over by the police before she got there. Not today. Not on her day.

The traffic lights seemed to be on her side and it wasn't long before she was pulling up into the parking lot of the church. Driving around she realised every parking spot had been taken. How inconsiderate! Yes she had turned up late, but they should have left her a parking space! She would have words with someone the next day about this.

Exiting the car park she drove down the road until she found a spot, nearly a block away. She got out of the car, cursing as her heels dug into the mud of the nature strip. Awkwardly she stormed up the footpath, the light rain again causing her makeup to run. It began to get into her eyes and she wiped them with the back of her hands, realising too late that she had probably just made things worse.

By the time she walked up the stairs to the church she was furious. Her hair and clothes were sodden and any earlier attempts she had made of improving her looks were rapidly undoing themselves. If she would have to give her speech looking like she had swum fully-clothed to the church, then so be it. The piece of her mind that she was going to give to all those inside had just grown a little larger.

Pushing the heavy doors open she stumbled into the foyer. An attendant standing there gave her a surprised look and hurried over.

"Would you like a service pamphlet?" he offered, fumbling with a pile of cardboard programs.

"I am absolutely drenched! Do I look like I need a pamphlet right now?" She bellowed, frowning with disbelief.

"No, of course not," he said nervously, accidentally dropping a few. He picked them up and rushed over to the sign-in table. He returned with a box of tissues. She grabbed a handful and started dabbing at her eyes. She was starting to blink now. Her mascara was a new one that she had only bought recently. She seemed to be having a reaction to it. The tissues she used were stained, like Rorschach ink blots. All that time she had spent doing her makeup, wasted. She threw them on the floor with disgust.

"Get out of my way," she said, pushing the small man aside. She slammed through the interior doors into the church.

The building was utterly intimidating and she stopped for a second to take it all in. The ceiling was stories high, painted with epic classical portrayals of violent bible scenes surrounded by countless angels. The gold borders shone brightly accentuating the colours. She could picture herself in one of these scenes, her suffering immortalised for all to see.

Rebecca's eyes slowly fell on the large crowd on both sides of the church. Most faces were looking back at her and the well-dressed man on the stage had paused mid-sentence. He cleared his throat and continued.

"He was one of the most generous people I have ever known. I am grateful for my time with him. He definitely enriched those around him and I feel that I am a better person for his brief role in my life," he said. Gradually everyone turned their attention back to him.

Of course, she thought. Everyone was going to focus on his charity work. On his deeds. On his accomplishments. Let's all just forget about the man that he truly was.

Picking up her courage, Rebecca stomped her way down the aisle towards the stage. She ascended the stairs, trying not to lose her balance and stood next to the man, glaring at him. His eyes opened wide and his chubby face reddened.

"Yes, well, I um… I just wanted to say that he was a good man and he will always be remembered for what he gave back to the community. Uh, thank you," the man said, gathering up his notes before hastily making his way down the stairs. A few people clapped politely and the crowd quietened. She had the stage.

Rebecca wiped her eyes. The lights seemed brighter than expected and she squinted.

'My ...'" she started. Her voice caught and she coughed into her hand. She grunted, trying to expel the frog in her throat. "My father was not the man that you all thought he is. Was. He… he never abused me in any physical way, I'm not saying that or anything."

People in the audience began to murmur and she could hear people tutting with disapproval.

"Hey! He was my father and I am going to have my say!" She yelled into the microphone, causing a ringing sound.

This seemed to cause even more of a stir in the crowd, some people turning around to speak to those behind them

"You don't know what I have been through! I have had a difficult life. It wasn't easy being the middle child. Yes, we were well off. Yes, he was kind when he spent time with us. But I had to compete with all the charities and all the functions and all the benefits ..."

Heads in the crowd were beginning to shake and she tried searching for faces she knew, but her eyes were filling with tears. She wiped them with her sleeves.

"He never had time for me! He didn't tell me he loved me enough," she said between sobs. "Even his death was selfishly sudden, like he couldn't even stay alive long enough to say goodbye to me." Everything she had memorised, her rehearsed list of grievances were eluding her now.

The grumbling in the crowd was getting louder and a few people were even standing up to leave.

"What about me?!" Rebecca screamed. "Why doesn't anyone care about how this affects me? You were never there, daddy!" Rebecca cried, turning to face the casket.

Her eyes blurred and she stared at the enlarged black and white photo. His face was smiling, as if amused by her tears. As if this scene she was creating was entertaining him. As if he was grinning inside the coffin. As if he still didn't care about how she felt.

The crowd was getting louder. Shouts echoed in the large wooden interior.

His face in the photo was grinning from ear to ear. It was young and handsome. It was a proud face. It was a warm and confident face. It was an unfamiliar face.

Rebecca's pulse began to race and her breathing became difficult. She groaned loudly. Her legs buckled beneath her and she used the lectern to lower herself to the floor, her mind reeling. She frowned, trying to remember.

The service was today, wasn't it?

7 It's For Your Own Good *by Adam Mitchell*

Author's note: Family always comes first. Until there's greed involved and an inheritance to consider. This won't end well.

*

It was a day with few redeeming features. The sun, for it surely must have been there, was filtered through several kilometres of oppressive cloud. Between them, the elements had concocted a reluctant wash of grey which descended from the low-slung skyline, filling the world from the top down. If it weren't for the cars, it was one of those days that you could believe you were living in monochrome.

Three figures stepped out of a blue Toyota into the car park of the Gladstone Hymes Surgery. From afar, one was busy, attentive, efficient. The other two, with a colour palette to match the day, were considered, concerned and slow. The three shuffled awkwardly across the rain-slick asphalt and through the automatic doors.

"It all seems such a terrible bother, Alison. I still don't really think we need…" began Audrey Young.

"Now Mum. We've been through this. Thomas is concerned about you, that's all. We both are." Alison Young smiled, entirely missing Audrey's thinly disguised grimace at the word 'Mum'.

Since Alison had married her only son four years previously, Audrey had always detested her familiarity. Of course, the thought of finally getting the grandchildren that she was resigned to never having was a source of joy. Yet, there was something in the way Alison moved, spoke, touched her arm when she made a point, which left Audrey ill at ease. She was, Audrey concluded, a walking agenda. The 'spirit and enthusiasm' which Thomas had spoken about so lovingly when

30

they were courting was, to Audrey, deliberate and insincere. She'd hoped she was wrong. She was fairly sure she wasn't.

"It's a formality really. Just a check-up. I'm having one too!" Alison chirped with practiced concern. "It's just good to keep an eye on everything. It's a big house for the two of you. I really don't know how you manage! So, we - well Thomas really - just thought we'd make sure you could…y'know carry on. Cope with it all." That smile again. "Isn't that right Dad?" she added.

Geoffrey Young was already inside his newspaper. A gentle introvert, he'd learnt to cope with life in his later years by disappearing into print. He knew whose company he enjoyed and, to them, he was an amiable and generous friend. For everybody else, he deployed his text armour, fending them off with a book or a newspaper. Geoffrey didn't claim to have the perception of his wife, but he knew he didn't like Alison very much. Her visits usually required a good hundred pages or so. He lowered The Times.

"S'pose." he muttered without looking at Alison.

Audrey tutted. She hated it when Alison did this. She would draw Geoffrey in, asking him questions - to which he either wasn't listening or wasn't interested - garner a response like a salesman making a close, then claim him as a staunch ally in future conversations.

"See Mum, just a quick mental health check-up is all it is. Nothing to worry about."

"But we both …" attempted Audrey. This time it was the receptionist who cut in.

"Mr and Mrs Young? Dr Datta will see you both now," she chirped. "Erm … you can go in after them if that's OK?" she added, seeing Alison rise with them. Alison slumped back into the faux-leather, reached for her phone, thumbed idly to

Facebook and waited.

After fifty minutes or so, the senior Youngs emerged from the consulting room, arm in arm.

"All good I hope?" quizzed Alison rhetorically, as she breezed past them and into the doctor's open door.

Audrey looked back towards the room, squeezed her husband's arm reassuringly and returned to the waiting area.

The consulting room was over-warm and clinically neat. The blinds, photograph frames, bookshelves and even the pens in their matt black holder looked like they had been scared into regimental conformity. Order was Dr Datta's comfort. He removed his glasses, placed them on the desk, nudged them gently until they were parallel to the edge and smiled at Alison Young like an old friend.

"Here for check-up then, Alison?" he offered with a smile. Dr Ranjit Datta spoke in the kind of lyrical, imperfect Indian-English which made it seem like he was putting on the Indian accent.

Alison half-smiled, distracted. "Oh sure…why not?"

Without breaking his bedside manner, the doctor leaned forwards. "So, we have…agreement still?" he questioned.

"We do. Five thousand now, the rest when they're…" she looked down at her hands, twitching her fingers, as if to flick away the last traces of conscience. "…rehomed."

"Good, good," replied the doctor, still smiling confidently. "Such a cruel thing is dementia. Can take most seemingly healthy people, so quick it is. So…random."

"Just make sure. It has to look like they can't cope but I don't want them to look like basket cases. They just need to be convinced that they'd be better off…somewhere where they're looked after properly. It's for their own good, really."

"Will look like needs to look. Paperwork, evidence. All is

good."

"Good."

"While you're here," added the doctor, "might as well give you check-up too? Make it seem…authentic? We start with memory test, yes?"

Alison sighed, "I guess they'd wonder why I was out so quickly. OK, let's get it done."

Twenty-five minutes later, Alison Young rose from her chair. Without speaking or looking the doctor in the eyes, she left the room. Behind her, the only remaining trace in the perfect order of Dr Datta's office was a vapour of overpriced perfume and a well filled envelope. Dr Datta looked down at his desk, straightened the envelope and continued to smile.

The regimented, terracotta rooftops of suburbia gazed longingly up towards the sky. Their TV aerial hands and chimney stack fingers pointed skywards and beckoned like children gazing at fireworks. Suburbia; the most divisive region on the planet. The Gaza Strip of the middle classes. Hedges were clipped, windows washed, driveways edged, cars cleaned. To some, born with a parentally pre-loaded vision of their future selves, it was an aspiration. A respectable end-stop of predictable comfort. To others, it was a grid work of soul-sucking, mundane familiarity. For ten years, to Thomas, it had been home. For four years, to Alison, it had simply never been enough.

"All I'm saying is it'll sound better coming from you, Thomas." Alison was in a calm yet formidable mood. Thomas knew this because she was using his name in almost every sentence.

It was strange how hearing her use his name had transformed over time. Initially, it had been used gently, like the many pet names he'd had for her; to reinforce sincerity and suggest a deeper, comforting level of intimacy. Now it was less 'used', more 'wielded'. A blunt weapon to enforce clarity, attention or dominance. In the quiet evenings when Alison was out with her friends at God knows where, Thomas took out their letters and the many photographs from the early days of their relationship. He looked into the eyes of the two static figures and tried to flesh them out. To resuscitate the moments which had so enchanted him and recapture the hopeful joy of that time. Each time the ritual had a similar outcome. Anxieties and insecurities which began in his stomach, worked their insidious path up to his chest and then invaded his head. As he looked into the eyes of the lovers before him, he just couldn't help but wonder. Had he loved her more than she him? Did he really know her?

"I get it," he replied, "It's just …"

"Oh, Thomas!" snapped Alison, on the verge of losing her calm, "We've been over this so many times. And Datta's got the money now. I know it seems cruel, but it's only bringing forward the inevitable. It's for their own good, you know that. Don't you Thomas?"

Thomas sighed. He was weary of the whole situation now and just wanted it over. The sleeplessness, the anxiety was constant and loomed over him as heavy and grey as the oppressive sky outside.

"So, as soon as he's written the report, yes? Datta said we can have it whenever we want, but we'll probably have to give it a week to make it look convincing." Alison touched his arm gently. Thomas felt like he was being shackled.

"Yes," was all he could manage.

The following Tuesday arrived clearer and fresher than the previous week had been. As though the sky had coughed and cleared its chest. In the living room of his parental home, Thomas sat on the edge of the memory-soaked leather sofa he'd so loved as a child. There was no comfort there now. The solemnity of his face was matched by the atmosphere in the room. It was sickly and tormented. Thomas struggled to look at his parents.

"Mum, please don't cry. It's…for the best. The doctor said that with support and full-time care you could be fine for… for years. But you can't be expected to manage this house any more. It's too much. I'm sorry Mum, Dad. I'm so sorry."

Alison was holding Thomas's hand like a frightened child. Which was precisely what he was. Sensing a weakness, she stepped in.

"Mum, Dad, you know we'll look after this place. Thomas has so many memories here. He can't wait to be back again. The doctor only has your best interests at heart, and it's what he strongly recommended. And, of course, we'll let you choose the…place, you decide to go. There's some lovely ones out there, gardens and libraries and everything. And you'll be looked after. It's a new start, that's all."

Audrey was tearfully silent; shoulders bobbing, exuding defeat. For once, Geoffrey was the one to break the silence. This time there was no book, no newspaper to put down. He stared directly at Alison in a way which she'd never seen before. A gaze full of intent and defiance. What he said was unexpected to all in the room.

"Alright Alison, Thomas. We'll start making preparations immediately. Thank you for your concern and advice." With an effort, he struggled to his feet, placed a hand gently on Audrey's shoulder, and quietly left the room.

"Lovely! I'll put the kettle on then shall I, Mum?" breezed Alison, "I think we all need a cup of tea."

Thomas moved across and sat next to his mother. He placed an arm around her and gently pulled her tear-stained face onto his shoulder. The protected now the protector.

Two months later the blue Toyota crunched slowly into a gravelled driveway, the imposing Georgian frontage of the approaching building slowly peeped out from behind the retreating hedges. The four Youngs stepped out and entered the building. Alison was the only one to speak.

"Looks lovely! Well done you two!"

In the impressive foyer, they were met by a smiling man wearing a mid-blue suit and an air of confidence.

"Ah, Mr and Mrs Young. And Mr and Mrs Young, ha-ha!" he chuckled, "All the paperwork's been sent through by Dr Datta. Everything's in order for an immediate ... erm ... admission."

"That's very good to hear, Peter." Thomas spoke with unusual clarity and assertiveness as he shook their host by the hand. Alison was jarred by his confidence, but immediately put it down to his nerves and overcompensation.

Turning to face Alison, Dr Peter Johannsen addressed her in calm tones, gently touching her arm.

"So, Mrs Young, Alison, it's going to be a pleasure to have you here. Yours is an ... ah ... unusual case, however, you're in good hands. I'm sure we can make some excellent progress. If you'd care to step this way, Thomas kindly dropped off your belongings earlier in the week, so it should feel just like home."

Alison had not gone quietly, it had taken four assistants to 'process her admission'. As she had desperately screamed his name, Thomas had felt all the anxieties of those nights alone ebb away. Pulling away from the Bailsworth Acute Psychiatric Admission Centre, the car was filled with a rich, peaceful silence. Audrey Young gazed out of the back window, her hand on her husband's arm.

"Ah, well. That's that then. It's for her own good."

8 Betrayal in Java *by Allan Carter*

Author's note: An Australian businessman's trip to Indonesia has an unexpected outcome.

*

He was about to have breakfast. Before doing so, he looked down from the apartment window at the scene below. There was a commotion beside the rubbish-filled canal. Two people were lifting a blue and bloated body onto the pavement. Breakfast no longer seemed attractive.

He had been in Jakarta for three days. The apartment belonged to a relative. On the fourteenth floor were swimming pools, a kiosk and numerous benches. People walked and sat in the fetid air. Children splashed each other in the shallow pools. A hum of distant traffic floated over the walls.

Mutiara sat in the shade waiting for him. As he approached, he thought how the hijab actually added to Mutiara's beauty. When he had first visited Indonesia, few women had worn the hijab; now almost all women did.

He wondered about the shift in the practice of Islam that had ensured such conformity. To him, it was regrettable that so many attractive heads were now covered, but he had to concede that the woman in front of him was no less attractive because of her headscarf.

"*Selamat pagi,*" he said in his Australian accent.

"Good morning, Jeremy," Mutiara replied in almost faultless English. "What's the plan?"

"The plan is to have breakfast. My hunger was stopped in its tracks when I saw a body being lifted from the canal. Let's go down to the food court."

They took the lift to the ground floor where all types of food was on offer. Jeremy opted for *nasi goreng*, the only

Indonesian dish he found palatable. His companion went for something much spicier.

As he watched Mutiara eating, Jeremy thought about how she had approached him in a hotel foyer where he was meeting a local delegation. She had been very friendly and had offered to escort him around the city and show him places he had probably never seen. He had taken up this offer because he needed to fill in a week or so before attending a conference in Bogor.

Breakfast completed, they walked slowly through the lobby to where the traffic drifted haphazardly along the busy thoroughfare. There was little observance of lanes, but the pace was so slow it didn't really matter. Jakarta had been close to gridlock for several years and, as the tollways were expensive, none but the rich would use them.

They decided to walk, with Mutiara pointing out key features of the city. At one point there was a monument to some generals who had been murdered in the 1965 coup. Jeremy walked over to inspect it more closely but was suddenly aware of several men shouting at him angrily. Jeremy was puzzled. What had he done?

Mutiara came closer. "Take off your shoes," she said hastily. "This is regarded as holy ground and you are causing offence."

Jeremy began to remove his shoes, but then he hesitated. He decided to move away. The men's anger had put him off.

They found a coffee shop in a large, modern shopping mall. Jeremy had noticed on this visit the contradictions. Modern shopping centres, hotels and apartments were being built expansively in a country where poverty and corruption were still the rule. Alongside the canals and railway lines, people lived in shacks made from scrap wood and iron mixed with cardboard walls. Children wandered on the roadways, trying to sell bottled water, or cigarettes.

"Those men were rather aggressive," Jeremy observed to his companion.

"Well, to them you are a *bule* – a foreigner- and some Muslims are getting very antagonistic towards those they call infidels. There has been an increase in militant action against bars and clubs where foreigners gather to drink and women are scantily dressed and wear lots of make-up. To a traditional Muslim, these things are morally wrong."

"So much for tolerance," Jeremy remarked.

Mutiara quickly changed the subject. "We could visit the aquarium," she suggested. "The place is cool and there are some excellent specimens, including piranha."

"Sounds good," Jeremy smiled and pushed a strand of hair back under her head-scarf.

They spent a pleasant few hours at the aquarium before returning to the lobby of the building where Jeremy had his apartment. Mutiara did not stay but agreed to go with Jeremy to a club that night at one of the spots frequented by tourists. Some hours later, Mutiara joined Jeremy. He drank beer; she sipped mineral water. It was difficult to converse in the noisy atmosphere and Jeremy used this as an excuse to get closer to Mutiara and whisper in her ear. She had not worn the hijab so her hair hung loosely about her shoulders. Her dress was fairly modest, but when she crossed her legs a tantalising expanse of thigh was exposed.

Suddenly there was the sound of breaking glass. Several men wearing head-bands and carrying long sticks rushed in and began smashing the drink bottles behind the bar. Shards of glass scattered across the floor and people ducked behind chairs to avoid being hit. Some men picked up chairs to defend themselves. Others pushed their female companions behind them for protection. However, most of the occupants of the bar either sat stunned, or ran for cover. They were obviously outnumbered. Then the men grabbed several women, including Mutiara, and dragged them out the door. Jeremy held Mutiara's hand for as long as he could, but she was pulled from his grasp, and along with the other women, herded through the door into a waiting van. The men who had lost partners looked around in confusion. Not long after, the police arrived, but they were not helpful and talked to the owner more than anyone else.

Jeremy had no clue about where to look for Mutiara. He did not know where she lived or if she had a job. All he could do was go back to the apartment and wait.

Mutiara entered the room adjoining the mosque and bowed respectfully toward an elderly, bearded man sitting cross-legged on the floor. An open copy of the Koran was in front of him. He continued to read for a few moments, then he looked up.

"You are all right?" he asked kindly. "The people who raided the club treated you well?"

Mutiara replied in High Javanese. "It went well. He suspected nothing. I was taken away, just like the others, and to him it would have appeared that I had been treated the same as everyone else."

"Do you think he is ready?"

Mutiara bowed her head. "In a day or two, we can accomplish our mission."

"Just remember to keep yourself pure," the imam advised.

"I will. He has done nothing improper, and I do not stay with him alone in his apartment."

"Just focus on your mission." The imam laid a hand on the open Koran. "It must be done soon. Our war against the infidels must not falter. Bless you, my child."

The elderly imam raised his hand in dismissal Mutiara backed towards the door, bowed, and left.

The next morning, Mutiara phoned Jeremy from the ground floor of his apartment building. A few minutes later, he met her. He noticed that her body was completely covered.

"I am so relieved to see you. Are you OK?"

"Fine. They let me go after a lecture about modesty and how women disrespect men if they show any flesh at all, except for the face and hands. My lipstick was wiped off and I had to wash my face. Otherwise, no harm done."

"Sometimes I think this country is primitive."

"It is better to respect cultures and try not to impose Western values on an Asian setting. Come, I want to take you to a beautiful part of the coast. We can have a lovely day relaxing."

With that, Mutiara took him to a car park where an attendant handed her a key and directed them to a late model car. She signalled for Jeremy to get in and Mutiara occupied the driver's seat. Before long, they entered the slipstream of Jakartan traffic. Jeremy could not believe the noise and the way cars weaved from one lane to the other; anywhere there seemed to be a space. Every time that the car stopped, boys would appear selling bottles of water, or cigarettes. At the side of the road, near an overpass, there was an old man with a monkey on a chain. The monkey danced, and drivers were expected to throw coins into a cup.

The road ahead seemed blocked. Smoke was rising from a group of cars, and flags and banners were being waved above the tops of the cars. People were rushing in all directions, some carrying banners. There was no sign of any police and the crowd seemed highly agitated.

"What's going on?" Jeremy asked.

"Must be a demonstration. There have been a few lately," Mutiara answered.

"What's the problem?"

Mutiara replied: "It's part of what we call *perjuangan* – a struggle. First, it was the struggle against the Dutch; then the struggle for independence. In 1965, it was the struggle against the Communists, and now it's the struggle to retain religious purity in the face of increasing secularisation, materialism and Western influences."

Jeremy shrugged. "You mean modernisation?"

"That's part of it, yes. But it's also because many Muslims fear that their faith is being undermined and that Islam needs to undergo a process of renewal."

Jeremy frowned. "It seems as if this renewal, as you call it, is often violent and has given rise to terrorism and economic disruption."

"Well, to some it is a *jihad* – a holy war, and the only valid result is a restoration of Islamic values."

Mutiara eased the car into a side street.

"I know a way out," she said confidently, as she slowly avoided street hawkers and motor-scooters. Jeremy was surprised at the number of people and the amount of activity evident in such a narrow passageway. However, he also noticed that many windows were boarded up.

After a few minutes, the road became less crowded. More and more people were on foot, carrying baskets or simply trudging along with no particular intent. Increasingly, rice-fields appeared on both sides of the road. Every patch of arable land had something growing on it. Dwellings were ramshackle, but those who sat on their haunches in the front of them smiled and waved as the car passed. Jeremy had read somewhere that the poorest people were the happiest, and he was beginning to believe it.

A while later, the sea became visible. Some boats were a little way out, their occupants probably fishing. Other boats rested on the sand with nets draped over their prows. Mutiara kept driving until they stopped at a picturesque spot. They moved away from the car.

The beach was secluded. They walked along the sand until they came to a clump of coconut palms. Mutiara said, "Look at the sea, Jeremy. I love it here because it is such a quiet place in a very crowded island. Step forward and take in the view." She moved behind him, raising her arm as she did so.

Two men appeared quickly. One held Jeremy and the other slashed his throat with one stroke.

Mutiara continued to look out at the gently moving water. She ignored the activity behind her as the two men carried the body away. After several minutes, she turned and headed back towards the car. In the distance she saw the imam and two attendants looking down at the beach. A shiver of remorse passed through Mutiara. She could not look directly at the imam and when she reached her car, she slumped into the driver's seat and gripped the steering wheel until her knuckles turned white.

Jeremy was reported missing, but was never found.

A few days later, a lone seabird was flying above the Java Sea. It looked down to see a corpse, blue and bloated, rolling across the waves.

9 When We Were Young *by Mat Clarke*

Author's note: Love your brother. Love your sister. Love your family. But only if they don't piss you off.

*

Gregg put his hands on his hips, exhausted after the walk up the grassy slope. He looked down past his black polished shoes to the coffin being lowered into the rectangle pit where his brother was to spend eternity. The service had been short with barely any in attendance; five people including the priest. Everyone had left immediately afterward so that it was only the grave digger and himself witnessing the end of Ian Richards

Gregg thought back to when the two of them had been so young they had only just started thinking about girls. He had not yet realised also just how much he hated his brother. Or the short time it would take for this opinion to be formed. It had been his dream that his brother accept him and allow the two of them to become good friends, but he should have realised his brother was too much of an asshole to ever let that happen.

"Hey Ian," Gregg said to his brother, while watching him put on his sneakers by the door readying to go outside. "Where you going?"

"Not somewhere you can go. It's for grown-ups only."

Ian nodded, then thought for a moment before he said, "But, you're not a grown-up."

Ian stood to his full height. "I'm as tall as dad." Ian opened the front door. "You're not even as big as our neighbour's dog. So, stay." Ian laughed and headed up the driveway away from the family home.

Gregg's insides dropped and his eyes burned as he fought off tears. He turned on the television in an attempt to fill his

44

thoughts with something else so he could at least pretend he did not care.

Mum had baked biscuits and brownies this morning. Eating always made him feel better. Gregg got up from the couch and went to the pantry. On his way he thought of ways he might be able to get his brother to like him being around. Maybe if he brought all of Ian's friends something to eat, they would like him. Surely eating made them as happy as it made him. He grabbed a bag from the pantry and filled it with brownies and cookies. The ANZAC ones were so full of syrup and still soft and warm from today's bake that they melted in the mouth. Ian put the lot in a shopping bag and left the house on his bicycle.

He had written his name on the main horizontal support bar on his bicycle in a thick black marker. People in his street sometimes called out his name. Some were kids he didn't even know. He still wasn't sure if they were messing with him or were admiring his bike. What did it matter, as long as they knew this was his cool bike.

He rode until he reached the oval near their school and looked around, finally finding his brother and his friends sitting in the middle of the overgrown grass. No one looked up as Gregg rode to within a metre of his brother and stopped. He took out the shopping bag and opened it. The aroma of freshly baked cookies filled the air.

"Oh hey, can I have one?" Tim said.

Lisa nudged Tim.

"Oh, and one for, Lisa."

Gregg smiled and handed out biscuits and brownies for everyone including his brother, who did not seem annoyed by the intrusion. Gregg then stared into the bag and wondered which he should choose for himself. It was exciting now that he had got his brother's approval.

Ian grabbed the bag out of Gregg's hand and smiled at his brother. "Thanks for bringing the food. Tell mum I'll be home later. You can go now."

The group laughed and went back to their conversations, forgetting that Gregg had ever been there at all. The chatting turned to who had been kissing who and what rated R movies they had watched.

His invisibility burned him, and for a moment he wished his brother would die from choking or getting food poisoning. Which would be silly, because then they would all die from food poisoning, even mum and dad. He thought about hanging around nearby, but Ian would eventually yell at him to go away anyway.

Gregg steered his bike around the way he had come and rode across the oval to the school and outdoor basketball courts. No one was around, so he practiced riding down and then up different sets of stairs, jumping his bike up onto seats and generally being radical. If his brother's friends took the time to get to know him, surely they would see how cool he was.

"Hey!" A man called out from the main office. The door was open behind him and showed the headmaster's desk, book cases, and large leather chair. A dreaded place Gregg never wanted to be sent to. A place where bad kids came back from with sore behinds. The old man wore a loose T-shirt and grey tracksuit pants. A kettle in his hand and a newspaper in the other.

Without looking to see if Gregg was going to stop riding on the outdoor furniture, the old man turned and went back into the office. Gregg shrugged. He had seen the old man cleaning the outdoor bins during the day, but why he was here on the weekend and in the headmaster's office, Gregg could only guess.

It was after lunch, and Gregg was hungry and wanted to go home anyway. He rode past the oval on his way and saw that Ian was sitting alone on the grass and eating the extra brownie and cookie from the bag. Gregg ignored him and instead thought of what mum might be cooking them for lunch.

"Hey!"

Gregg turned back to the school expecting to see the old man again. No one was at the office door and it was closed. He turned to the oval and saw that Ian was walking toward him. Ian yelled to Gregg again.

Gregg said, "What?"

"I've got something to show you."

Gregg thought about what Ian might show him, and then realised he probably just wanted to embarrass him again, or more likely punch him in the arm. He stayed and waited for what ridicule was to come. He liked his brother, so there had to be some way to make Ian like him back. Ian came over and punched Gregg in the upper arm, although lightly like he did with his other friends. Which was odd, because normally Ian tried to leave a bruise.

"I'll show you something," Ian said.

Gregg tried not to smile when he said yes, but it was impossible to hide his glee. Ian got on the back of Gregg's bike and pointed the way he wanted to go. It was hard riding and balancing at first, but once he got up to speed he was able to ride without wobbling.

"No, wrong way," Ian said. "Back to the school."

Gregg did as he was told, although in a wide arc so they didn't tip over. They rode past the main office and arrived at another door that was only for the older kids' classrooms. If you tried to get in that way in the morning before school you would get a punch in the arm by one of the older kids guarding the door. The teachers never saw it happen, at least that was the way it seemed.

They stopped at the door. Ian got off and reached into his pocket to take out a key. He held it up high like it was a rare jewel, then put it in the keyhole and turned. The door opened. He looked over to Gregg, "Not bad, yeah?"

Gregg left his bike by the door and followed his brother inside. The excitement of being with his brother on a scary but fun adventure was almost more than he could handle. His bladder tightened and he felt so sick that he was sure he would puke.

Gregg almost burst out laughing when they passed by the teacher's office and saw there was trash and bottles everywhere. They were even bigger pigs than kids.

They approached a set of stairs leading down into the darkness.

"Down here," Ian said, and led the way.

Gregg nodded and followed his brother. Each of the wooden steps creaked with their own tune as if tapping keys on a piano. However, this tune was from a horror movie and it made his jaw hurt from clenching his teeth so hard. The smile had gone from his face, and he now preferred that they forget the adventure and go outside where it was lighter.

"Should we go back?" Gregg said.

Ian clicked on the light at the bottom of the stairs, and Gregg's fears disappeared - although not entirely.

"Over here," Ian said.

Ian went to a shelf underneath a dust and cobweb covered window well above his head, and grabbed hold of a crossbow that surely could not be real. It had no string on it where the arrows went, but it still looked cool.

"Let's go." Ian began back up the stairs.

With new found bravery, Gregg stayed and looked all around the room at the amazing things that were stored here. Maybe he would get something for himself as well?"

The door slammed shut and the light went off. Gregg spun back to the door and called his brother's name. He could hear laughing fading back up the steps.

"Don't leave me here!" Tears came in a flood and then he was banging on the door trying to turn the handle, but it stuck in place.

It took an hour of screaming before the old man came to let Gregg out. The janitor had tried to grab onto his shoulder, but Gregg had spun and scrambled up and out. His bike was gone and his brother as well. So he ran home.

It was many decades later at a once-yearly family get-together that Gregg, now 52, had reminded Ian about the day they had gone to the basement and how he had been locked down there with the light off. Ian barely remembered. So Gregg convinced his brother to return there and had taken ANZAC biscuits and brownies to make sure his brother recalled what had happened that day. The beers had been Ian's idea.

The same door was still there and still painted a dirty green. Gregg got through the padlock and chain with bolt cutters. Ian grinned, but said nothing.

Gregg took Ian to the same stairs and pointed out how he had been terrified when they had gone down, then more so upward after being let out by the janitor. Ian had laughed. "Yeah, good ol' days, hey?"

All the confiscated goods were gone from the shelves. The crossbow that Ian had taken had been noticed by a gun enthusiast friend. It was valued, restrung, readied for auction and sold for five figures.

They went back up the stairs with Ian still laughing.

Gregg told his brother how he had run home because his bike had "Oh, right, your bike," Ian said. "I rode that, but pranged it into a car backing out of a driveway. I couldn't hit the brake because of the crossbow. Lucky too, because dropping that thing would have cost me money. I never did go and try and steal your bike back from the Hollanbrook's. Boy were they mad about you wrecking the side of their new car. They kept calling your name as I ran away. Don't worry, I went back another day and calmed them down by telling them you were retarded."

Gregg punched the wall. It was solid concrete, an old fashioned solidly built school.

"You did what?" Gregg clenched his teeth. "I asked Belinda Hollanbrook out, but she had already stopped talking to me. Now I know why. I can't believe you're such an asshole."

Gregg grabbed hold of Ian's shoulder and pushed him backward toward the stairs. His brother tumbled over and down, landing on the concrete basement floor with such a loud crack that he had to have broken his leg. When Gregg reached the bottom of the stairs there was blood pouring out of his brother. His head had opened up, and his brain was exposed. Gregg called an ambulance, but upon their arrival they said he had died instantly. Gregg had wanted to hurt his brother, and had wished him dead many times. Now it was a reality. He had not told the police the true story, and instead had said that he had been helping his drunk brother up the steps when he had slipped and fallen.

"And that's how you get away with your murder," Gregg said to his brother's descending body. "And if I had the time over again, I would have pushed you even harder."

10 Snog, Marry or Kill *by Elly Parkinson*

Author's note: When a man has the destiny to kill, it's only a matter of time before he fulfils it. A story that focuses on whether we really have the free will we think we do or do we all have a pre-set destiny, even killers.

*

Please see our ebook for my story.
Thank you.

11. Changing Winds *by Jo Stanford*

Author's note: My story was inspired by my Dad who has been in the CFA for many years.

*

The cacophony of sound coming from the CFA pager demanded attention as it jiggled and danced on the outdoor table. Several conversations stopped mid-sentence as the alarm blasted for five long seconds. Eddie pressed the button to make it stop, but the collective relief lasted only until Eddie put down his three-year-old granddaughter and stood, declaring he had to go.

A chorus of voices mildly protested, the loudest of which was his wife Harriet's.

'Are you sure? Can't you let others handle this one? It's your birthday!'

'Tom and Jackie are out of town so they'll need me to drive the truck. There's thousands of campers around this weekend, they'll want a good turn out.'

'Where is it, Dad?' his oldest daughter asked.

'Towards the mountains to the east, about seven k's from here. They've called five brigades.'

Eddie's children and their spouses and grandchildren, as well as several dogs, milled around the long table under the shade of the dense mop-top tree, lazing away the warm afternoon. Homemade and home-grown morsels covered the table; dips, olives, crusty bread, juicy berries. Several of the grandchildren played cricket on the grass, hampered by one of the dogs occasionally stealing the dirty tennis ball.

It was early autumn, but still there were summer-like conditions in north eastern Victoria. The surrounding hills were a dry, pale, brown, and dotted with trees that drooped in exhaustion. A thirsty looking dam was surrounded by a small herd of dusty steers. Any small fire had the potential to be dangerous, and as much as Eddie's family lamented the need for him to leave his own birthday party, they understood.

Eddie moved as quickly as his ageing frame allowed, grabbed his car keys and wallet, and made the short drive to the station. He was right; although five other volunteers had arrived, there was no one who had the training and experience to drive the truck. Even though his eyesight was going and his reactions slower than they used to be, he was still their best driver.

'Happy birthday, Eddie.' Eddie's good friend and neighbour, Wally, shook his hand. 'Three quarters of a century!'

'Yep. Only twenty five years to go.'

'Are we still on for drinks tomorrow?'

'The club at five!'

'We'll be there. Hey, didn't you have your family coming today?'

'Yes. Hopefully I'll be back in time to eat the roast lamb we marinated overnight.'

'I'm sure they'll save you some,' Wally laughed.

Eddie changed into the heavy, fire resistant suit and hoisted himself awkwardly into the driver's seat of their almost brand new tanker. Years of dedication to fundraising and applying for grants by a small group of passionate community members had finally paid off. It was one of the small town's biggest collective achievements. Hard won, too, since Marion was still not speaking to John and poor Frank's heart attack at a CFA Auxiliary meeting was the talk of the town.

Eddie turned the key, delighting in the deep purr of the engine as it came to life. He waited the two minutes it took for the well-trained volunteers to pack provisions into the truck and jump in.

'Lights and sirens folks?' Eddie called out with a mischievous grin.

'Sure Eddie, why not. Let the town know we're on the job,' Wally called from the back seat. Eddie glanced down at the dash and flipped the lights and sirens on. This was definitely his favourite part of the job! Eddie's five-year-old inner self grinned as he steered the red fire engine onto the main road.

Pulling up the truck at the fire site, Eddie took in the smoky scene. Embers swirled overhead. A line of low flames stretched across the paddock, already a few hundred metres long. Not a big fire, but one that had potential, especially since the eucalypt covered foothills were close enough to make out the leaves swirling in the wind.

Seven trucks were there already and a swarm of yellow uniformed CFA volunteers moved busily in different directions, intent on the roles they'd trained for. Eddie jumped out of the truck. His heavy boots dropped onto the dusty soil, crunching on a clump of straw-coloured grass. He spotted the Incident Controller and approached, awaiting orders.

'Margaret Bay! Great, you've arrived. We need you on the east flank with Scottsdale. They're setting a fire break and backburn at the base of the hill over there. Hopefully it'll stay in the grass and we can aerial bomb it when the choppers get here. But we've gotta stop this thing from hitting the hills, or it'll be a whole other ball game.'

Eddie and his crew idled over the bumpy paddock towards the base of the hill. He had to stop a few times while billows of thick smoke blew over. He spotted flashes of another red engine and followed Scottsdale into the thicker bush. Eddie jumped out, reflecting on the relative serenity, but he knew it was an illusion.

'Scottsdale! How are you?' Eddie called as he shook hands

with the crew of the nearby truck. He'd never met any of them before, but that didn't matter; out there they were all best mates.

'Margaret Bay, thanks for backing up us. We thought they'd left us alone in the firing line.'

'No worries mate, happy to lend a hand.'

They set about clearing some scrub from either side of the track as the Scottsdale crew tended a small backburn designed to stop the march of a fire front as it ran out of fuel to burn.

'Hey Eddie, want a hand with that?' Wally quipped as Eddie grabbed an axe.

'No thanks Wally, I'm not too old to wield an axe just yet. Aren't you supposed to be laying out that hose?'

'Yes sir.'

'Where do you want me?' asked nineteen-year-old Trudy, the baby of the bunch. She was high on enthusiasm, but a little rash. She seemed too young, but it was a changing world and Eddie knew he was the dinosaur.

'OK Trudy, you're on hose. Dampen the area between the truck and the backburn, just in case this thing gets too close.'

An hour later, sweat dripped down Eddie's back, gravel sloshed under his eyelids and he could taste the smoke at the back of his nose. He was sitting in the truck, ordered in by Wally for a short break. They'd successfully held their ground. The bulk of the front was still heading south and they'd stalled the eastern flank. He drank warm water from a plastic drink bottle that tasted like kerosene and mud.

'Agh, yuck! There's gotta be a way to keep water cold here.'

He was contemplating the benefits of installing a fridge in the new truck when the sky darkened and people started yelling. A sudden south westerly was picking up and embers started showering the truck.

He grabbed the radio.

'Margaret Bay here, we've got incoming. Can we have back up?'

'Margaret Bay, copy that. We're sending tankers three in your direction, hold on.'

Ash rained so thick their uniforms turned deep grey. Wearing full personal protective gear, the Margaret Bay and Scottsdale crews stood side by side, hoses and shovels in hand, barely able to make out the person next to them and the trucks behind.

'Where's Elvis when you need him?' Trudy's older brother Jasper yelled as he looked up for the fire bomber helicopter.

'Probably too busy eating his peanut butter and jelly sandwich,' quipped Trudy.

A nearby tree burst into flames.

'Shit,' the siblings shouted in unison as they raised the hose.

It was no good. There was no point trying to be heroes.

Eddie called retreat.

'We're out of here. Drop and detach the hose. Get in, get in! '

Eddie jumped in the driver's seat, started the engine, threw the gear stick into reverse and turned the truck onto what he thought was the track.

But he couldn't see a thing through the black smoke and raining embers.

'Damn, damn, damn,' he whispered.

He was faced with the choice of driving into a tree or ditch, or waiting until they were burned-over by the approaching front. He peered out the windows frantically, crawling along at walking pace.

Another shrub burst into flames a few metres to his right. There was no escaping this fire now.

The protocol had been seared into his brain through years of training. He'd been lucky in that he'd never had to use it. Until now; with adrenalin running high, full personal protective gear slowing his movements and five other terrified volunteers looking to him for guidance.

He spoke clearly, precisely, hoping he sounded like he knew what he was doing. Hoping that he could alleviate at least some of the fear in the others, especially young Trudy and Jasper.

Under his direction, they sealed the cabin, turned on their emergency lights, relayed messages to the Incident Controller as per protocol and readied the fire blankets. All the while the air in the cabin was heating up, despite the air conditioner running on full blast.

Emergency sprinklers sprayed water over the truck but from within the cabin, the drips on the windows were barely visible in the thick darkness. As the crackle of flames escalated to a roar, the volunteers crouched under their fire blankets and breathed thick, hot air through their masks.

Eddie tried to catch Trudy's eyes in the flashes of light from the surrounding flames and truck lights. Her head was down, but he was relieved to see Jasper's arm around her shoulders.

As the air became so stifling he could barely complete a breath, his heartbeat pounded like a drum and his hips screamed in protest, a strange sense of calm descended. He decided with absolute certainty that they would all die.

Headlines flashed before his eyes; Six Die in Burnover, Brave Volunteers Sacrifice Lives. He hoped that his granddaughter would have at least a vague, fond memory of her Pop.

But as he was waiting for the windows to shatter and his skin to sear, Jasper shouted 'It's passing! We're gonna be OK!'

Eddie's heart gave a couple of extra heavy thumps in the realisation that Jasper was right. The noise had quietened slightly and the flashes of flames were less intense.

He moved his fire blanket and peeked out. Acrid air filled

the interior of the cabin, fumes rising from the plastics and upholstery. With relief he noticed that gaps were appearing through the billowing smoke outside the truck.

'Alright folks, it's time to get out of here.'

Eddie moved as quickly as his stiff hips would allow and exited the truck with gloved hands on the red-hot door handle. He removed his mask, breathed in the singed air and swallowed a rasping cough.

Everything was black; the bare ground, shrivelled bushes and tree trunks. High in the trees, leaves had turned brown but were still intact. He and Wally shared a knowing look. That was way too close for comfort, they were lucky to be alive.

'Everyone OK?' Eddie croaked through his raw throat. He patted Trudy's shoulder, 'You alright love?'

'Yeah,' she whispered, wide eyed.

Flashing lights caught his eye as another three firetrucks appeared. The rotating red beams eerily lit the blackened landscape. Dozens of firefighter volunteers jumped out of the trucks and surrounded the survivors, patting them on the backs, shaking their hands.

Eddie asked about Scottsdale. They'd escaped the brunt of the fire front and were all OK. For once, he enjoyed being the centre of attention and was silently pleased when the Incident Controller singled him out and shook his still trembling hand.

'I believe it's your birthday,' he said.

Eddie nodded.

'Well, I think it's you who's been giving out the presents. These young recruits were lucky to have you around. You can drive my truck any time, Eddie.'

'Thank you, sir.'

'I believe it's drinks at the club tomorrow?'

'Yes, you're welcome to come.'

'I think you'll find a few of us happy to take up the invitation!'

Two hours later, Eddie had showered and was sitting back at the table in the garden with his children and grandchildren, beer in hand, the stench of smoke still in his nostrils.

Harriet called them for a late dinner. 'Imagine having to go out to a fire on your birthday! No rest for the wicked. Did they put it out safely, love?'

'Yep, no problem.'

'That's good. But why you don't retire and leave it to the young ones is beyond me.'

Eddie smiled and winked at his youngest granddaughter, who had crawled up onto his lap again.

'Maybe one day.'

12 Pyrrhic Victory *by Chun Kiu Ng*

Author's note: Every generation has witnessed their share of calamities that have shaped the course of history. Rowan always believed that a greater calling awaited him. Now, he answers its call alongside his brothers in arms as the full wrath of a kingdom descends upon the traitorous Midlands. For good or for ill, Rowan must decide on where he shall stand – or fall – in the tumultuous times following That Day."

*

Rowan kept a firm hand on his reigns as one last volley of fire pots streaked across the sky. Their black tails joined the blanket of smoke rising from the besieged city. Battle horns heralding their arrival like the deep tolls of the great belltowers of High Arichis. The Crusaders of the Church of Valor had finally joined the fray.

The engineers cheered them forward with raised fists from their hastily constructed siege engines as Rowan and his brethren charged down the final stretch of open field towards Lunatas.

The most senior of Paladins led the charge of the heavy cavalry straight towards the pulverised city gates. It was unfortunate that the once great city from the days of the First Empire had to be destroyed but there would be no stopping the wrath of Setonia's armies.

Horns sounded above the thunderous charge and the light cavalry peeled away from the main column. Rowan had to fight the urge to stay with the main column into the depths of the viper's nest. Fortunately, his steed had better sense than he and followed the rest of his company.

As they rode, regulars from the army formed up to the sound of drums, ready and waiting to follow them into the city.

Rowan brandished his spear high into the air. His captain led them through a sizeable breach in the walls. The riders closed ranks to four abreast to pass through the rubble.

Rowan found himself screaming at the top of his lungs in a rising chorus of voices as they passed the threshold of the crumbling walls. The stench of burning pitch assaulted his senses. It felt like someone had shoved his face into the heart of a smith's furnace. His eyes watered as he fought to keep them open against the acrid smoke. Burning wooden barricades were everywhere and Rowan could do nothing but follow the riders ahead of him. A voice cut through the cacophony of thunderous hooves, jangling mail and battle cries.

'Incoming!'

An arcing ball of fire struck a mere two ranks in front of Rowan into a waist high wooden barricade. Rowan pulled hard on the reigns to wheel his horse around and raised his shield against the flaming explosion. Rowan couldn't hear his own primal shout as searing heat washed over him.

Rowan's horse reared on its hind legs as a horse galloped into the mass of riders behind him, its mane awash with fire. Caught in the stirrups, its rider writhed in flames as he was dragged across the cobbled streets. The inferno around Rowan was nothing compared to the unlucky rider's chilling screams of agony – never mind the stench of burning flesh.

Rowan could hear the sound of battle and death cries of man and beast ahead. What was supposed to be an unstoppable charge had ground to a halt as the burning barricade churned a dark suffocating blanket of pitch over them.

Rowan saw the same look in the eyes of his brothers around him as they came face to face with their own mortalities. Icy hands reached their way for Rowan's heart. He knew his enemy and he would not bow to it.

'For Valor!' Rowan screamed at the top of his lungs and spurred his horse forward into the flames. He prayed for Valor for courage – for strength – for glory. He would show his instructors that their faith in him was not misplaced, that he did indeed possess a spark of Valor's spirit.

Rowan took a deep breath just before his horse lurched up into the air. As he felt the jolt of his horse landing, the saddle fell out from underneath him. Ground and sky tumbled to become one before he landed on cobblestone. One look was all it took for him to recognise the killing ground before him. Wooden stakes and obstacles scattered the wide street. Felled mounts and riders alike were a scattered mess as more barricades and burning buildings funnelled them into the missile storm from the far end of the street.

Rowan rolled to the side of the street as the riders who had followed him charged unwittingly into the chaos. He watched in horror as they too became trapped in the maze of bodies. Unwilling to ride down their own brothers, the build-up of riders made them sitting targets.

Rowan saw a ball of flame materialise at the end of the street. 'No!' he screamed, leaping to his feet. There was nothing he could do as the streaking comet consumed a dozen men and their mounts before his eyes.

Rowan clenched his jaw and his eyes steeled at the distant figure. By Valor, that sorcerer was going to pay.

An arrow ricocheted off the ground nearby and Rowan raised his shield, looking for some sort of cover. Not far away, men huddled behind the obstructions littering the street. Rowan ran over and nudged one in the leg. 'We have to move!'

'It's suicide!' the man replied, his voice breaking.

'Listen to me! Sons of Valor!' Rowan said as loud as he could to draw their attention away from the carnage ahead.

'Upon this day, we have been called to confront the Betrayer's corruption. Many have prayed for a calling such as this, yet it is us who have been given this divine task. Find the spark of Valor within yourselves and show the world that we are the light that will drive out this darkness!'

Rowan's eyes met with as many as he could. With a glance, he knew who were with him and who were not. 'We have to clear that fortification. Those that stay, get our brothers to dismount and find a way around. The rest of you follow me and Valor be witness to your deeds this day!'

Rowan charged towards the entrance of a burning building. *Valor protect me and give me strength.*

Putting all his weight behind his shield, he rammed it against the door. Weakened by the flames, the door's barricades failed. He was virtually blind as he rushed his way through the burning building. A break in the smoke gave him vision of a door leading outside.

'This way! Quick as you can!' Rowan choked as searing air scorched his throat and nostrils. His spirits were lifted to hear other voices behind him.

The heat subsided as he reached the back door. Finding himself in a narrow alleyway, he breathed a sigh of relief and turned around. A dozen soot covered faces looked to him. Their white and red tunics almost scorched beyond recognition.

He gave them a nod and began weaving through the cramped alleyway towards their goal. While muffled by the buildings, he could still hear the cries of his brothers' overhead which drove him to move even faster.

Turning a corner, he came face to face with a Marauder armed with a sword. Rowan cursed as he tried to bring his spear to bear, only for it to get trapped against the confines of the alley wall.

64

It was all the time the Marauder needed to raise his horn and blast a single note before Rowan ran his spear through the Marauder's chest. It proved to be a mistake as it lodged itself in the Marauder's ribcage. No matter, it was poorly suited for such cramped spaces.

'Stay alert!' Rowan said and drew his sword. They had barely gone a hundred feet before they ran into a patrolling band of Marauders. Alarm horns sounded as Rowan rushed to close the gap. A stout Marauder met him with a raised axe. They clashed violently, both unable to use their weapons effectively as the press of bodies forced them into a shoving match.

'Archers above!' someone called behind him.

Rowan could do nothing as several figures appeared on the rooftops, arrows already nocked to their bowstrings. He abandoned his shield and pressed himself against the wall, letting shield and Marauder fall past.

With his now free hand, Rowan gripped his sword halfway down its blade. He whipped his pommel up and drove his sword's hilt into the face of the second Marauder and stabbing the blade into a third, Rowan kept moving forward, pressing his advantage in the chaos of close combat where he used every inch of his blade to maim, injure and kill. He entrusted his brothers to finish off the Marauders who didn't die outright.

The final Marauder armed with a knife tried to tackle Rowan to the ground. Rowan pivoted and held the Marauder for his brother to stab in the back. Rowan saw two of his brothers still with spears launch them towards the archers, driving them away.

How these petty bandits had managed to occupy Lunatas for over three centuries was beyond him.

'Keep moving forward!' Rowan said.

They wound their way through a series of empty buildings

and found themselves in an open square. All four streets leading in were barricaded.

None of the Marauder's manning the fortifications appeared to have noticed them. Rowan signalled half his brothers to take the eastern side while the rest would follow him to the northern side.

They moved in a fast jog across the open ground, hastening into a sprint as they were spotted. With no shield to protect him, Rowan led the charge into the ranks of Marauders with only his armour to protect him. An arrow pierced his mail shirt but was stopped by his gambeson beneath. Another glanced off his helmet as he turned his head. Then, he and his fellow Crusaders were upon them. A short and vicious melee ensued as the Marauders were criminally unprepared for close quarter combat with little in terms of arms and armour. Some of them had nothing but their bows and slings, yet they resisted. Their perseverance paid off, managing to swarm one of his brothers before they too joined the ranks of the dead.

Rowan felt reinvigorated as he mete out justice for his fallen brother, yet there was no sorcerer to be found here. Likewise, his brothers to the east appeared to have no trouble dispatching the Marauders.

It was to the west that Rowan spotted a shirtless man ushering the remaining Marauders to the safety of the southern barricade. 'Tell Vala I did all I could, now go!'

'Don't let them get away!' Rowan said, pointing his sword to the fleeing Marauders.

The shirtless man's very skin radiated an unnatural light as he intercepted Rowan and his Crusaders at the centre of the square. There was only one explanation.

Sorcerer.

Flames seeped out of the man's pores and covered him

like a living coat of armour. Even his face was encased in a seemingly solid helm of shifting fire. A small ball of fire shot out the sorcerer's outstretched palm, leaving a smoking hole in the back of Rowan's brothers pursuing the retreating Marauders. The rest of the Crusaders turned to face the true threat.

A Crusader moved in to attack the sorcerer's exposed back. Flames violently unleashed from the sorcerer's back, leaving the Crusader clutching his blackened face. A halberd of living flame formed in the sorcerer's hands, ending the Crusader's misery.

Each of the Crusader's tried to exploit an opening but it was a fatal gamble every time. Another Crusader fell as he learned the hard way that their wooden shield meant nothing against the sorcerer's weapon. Not only did they have to contend with the weapon's physical shape but also the flames it would conjure out. Rowan himself was barely able to parry a thrust and avoid the stream of fire from its tip. His sword was left glowing red hot from the encounter.

Rowan didn't know what game the sorcerer was playing at, knowing full well his destructive capabilities. Were they being toyed with? The sorcerer had thwarted their attacks and had slowly whittled them down to five. The four times they had managed to land a glancing blow, they were rebuked by fire and only one of them had survived the feat.

'Reinforcements are coming!' one of his brothers said.

The sorcerer's head eerily tilted to the side, as Crusaders had finally managed to navigate their way through the defences.

The sorcerer burst into an embodiment of living fire as more heat washed over Rowan's numb face.

'He's going rampant!' one of the Crusader's said and ran for his life. The other three were only a step behind as they scattered in all directions. Everyone knew the tales of rampant sorcerers, capable of wiping out entire villages in their last suicidal act of pure madness.

The dread of knowing what could happen spurred him into action. Rowan had sworn by Valor that he would stop the sorcerer – even if it was the last thing he did.

'FOR VALOR!' Rowan yelled, entering a suicidal charge against the sorcerer. His shout turned to a scream of pain as he closed. The sorcerer raised his arms as like a bird flexing its wings before Rowan lowered his eyes away from the intense heat and thrusted his sword.

Light and sound overwhelmed his senses. A peaceful stillness took him. An unknowable freedom as all mortal concerns left his mind. He was unshackled and unburdened here. It lasted for an instant until he felt himself falling.

Rowan jolted awake to find him being held down. He fought against his restraints and a great weight on his body.

'By Valor, he's still alive – he's alive!' someone shouted painfully in his ear.

It took Rowan several long moments to get his bearings. Unknown faces slowly began to make sense. Crusaders. They were his brothers.

'Are you hurt? Can you stand?' a Crusader said.

Rowan nodded and they helped get him on his feet – an act which caused a cheer from what must have been a hundred men around him. There was a sudden hush as the crowd of men parted to make way for someone.

Rowan couldn't believe his eyes as a Bishop made his way forward for *him*.

'What is your name, young Crusader?' the Bishop asked.

'Rowan, Your Excellency,' Rowan said lowering his head.

'Well, Crusader Rowan, I do believe you have a bright future ahead amongst the Paladin ranks. Only a true follower of Valor could have accomplished a feat such as yours.'

'I'm – I'm honoured, Your Excellency,' Rowan said, not quite able to comprehend the fact. Had his years of hard work, study and prayers finally been heard? Most spent their entire lives without ever being graced with Valor's light.

The Bishop smiled warmly and patted his shoulder. 'He needs time to rest. See him to the healers.' The Bishop turned and moved towards the row of burning buildings. 'The rest of you, find a way through this damned thing and let nothing stop your righteous path.'

Rowan was certain he fainted several times as two of his brothers supported him all the way to the rear. He declined to ride or a stretcher as there were likely more of his brothers worse than he. They left him in the capable hands of the healers from the Church of Aria who tended to his injuries and burns.

'I'm sorry if this stings,' the young healer said as she applied an ointment to his skin.

Rowan couldn't feel a thing. The healer moved on to other patients soon enough, leaving him to watch smoke rise from deeper within the city. Every so often, there was a burst or flash of light that punctuated itself against the dark smoke.

'Just how many sorcerers are in there?' a passing soldier from the army said to his injured compatriot. They stopped as there was another flash of light from the city. 'Look, there goes another.'

'Good riddance the lot of them,' the injured soldier said and spat a thick wad of saliva into the ground. 'There'd be even more holed up in there if we didn't torch the Midlands and force them out.'

'You were in the first wave?'

'Yeah, Second Light Cavalry Regiment or what's left of it. Easier to fight those bastards in open ground. Best is when you catch them with the fleeing peasants. You know, kill two birds with one stone. See, they don't cut loose those dead weights nor can they fight proper with them around.'

'That's a bit harsh. I mean, they live in the Borderlands and all that, but...'

'Have you ever *seen* the Marauders fight? And I don't mean a random peasant with a knife. I mean the ones in actual armour as good as yours and mine with axes, maces and halberds. They pulverised our infantry ranks like they were nothing.'

'Still, it doesn't look like they'll last the night, especially when the Storm Riders of Atlanta get here.'

'They've mobilised? Hah! It's done then! Let them all burn. The Marauders are finished and Lunatas back to a ruin with them.'

A growing wave of nausea consumed Rowan as the heat of battle no longer clouded his mind. Peace and quiet brought an all too damning mirror of clarity against him. What had he done? Just who exactly had he defeated this day?

13 Live Free or Die *by Angelique Benoit*

Author's note: In a futuristic world with no freedom, an unlikely duo takes a stand. Where friendship and courage meet -there is always hope.

*

Please see our ebook for my story.
Thank you.

14 Mr Ex *by Dean MacAllister*

Author's note: Mr Ex has made some terrible decisions in his life, some of which have caught up with him.
This story answers the question: Are there worse fates than death?

*

On a cold, overcast Sunday afternoon a shiny, black Chrysler drove through an abandoned industrial area, before pulling up outside of an old brick factory. The driver got out and promptly opened up a rear car door. A pair of shiny Italian shoes emerged and planted themselves on the gravel driveway. The man they were attached to stood up and adjusted his expensive, tailored pin-striped suit. He ran his fingers back through his oily black hair and adjusted his sunglasses. Two men, dressed in dark suits, both tall and muscular, exited the car and stood behind him.

He smiled and looked up at the building. "It's good to be back home, boys."

They opened the door and entered. The building was large and mostly empty space, with a few crates stacked against a wall. Their footsteps echoed as they made their way to the back of the building, where there was a mezzanine working area, two floors of offices where he ran his business from. During the week these offices were usually full of goons yelling threats into phones, but today, besides a few men to guard the place and his armed entourage, the building was deserted. Despite the size everything was clean, from the plastered walls to the polished concrete floor. He strode towards his office, his men in tow.

Opening his door he paused, looking over his shoulder.

"You guys can take the rest of the day off."

"You sure, boss?" One of the men asked.

"Yeah, of course. You guys did good today. Go spend some time with your families. I'll call you if I need you, but we don't have anything important scheduled until Tuesday."

The men looked at each other and one of them shrugged.

"Ok boss. Thanks. We'll see you later."

They turned and headed towards the exit.

He watched them leave, before entering his office and switching on the lights.

"Wow, did I have a big week!" he said, removing his jacket and hanging it on a hook. His office was impressive in size and design. Despite owning an over-sized expensive desk, leather couches and mahogany bookshelves, he had opted to keep the concrete floor uncarpeted. Most of the other offices were carpeted, but he had instead used rugs beneath the seats and couches to make the office comfortable. Grabbing a crystal bottle of cognac and a glass, he walked around his desk and sat down in his executive-style chair, taking his sunglasses and shoes off. He poured himself a generous glass and chuckled.

"You should have seen it! I don't know who they were expecting, but they weren't expecting Mr Chilinski himself! You should have seen their faces! They barely even put up a fight. One guy was even apologising to me as I was beating him. Apologising!" he laughed. Nearly choking on his cognac, he coughed into his fist. He noticed a few drops of blood on his cuff. His smile vaporised.

"God damn it! This was a gift! If I find out which one of those lousy crack-heads bled on my French-cuffs, I'm going to feed him this shirt!"

He licked his thumb and started scratching at the stain. It wasn't coming out. He sighed, his cheerful mood destroyed. Turning his chair around, he stared at the large cube against the wall. It was the height of his desk and nearly as wide, covered with a black, silk sheet. Grabbing a corner of the sheet, he tugged it and it fell to the ground, revealing a steel animal cage. It was mostly empty, except for the clothed torso of a man lying face-down on the floor.

He downed the last of his drink and topped up his glass, placing his feet up on the corner of the cage. He leered down at the limp torso, sipping his drink. "Ahem!"

The torso stirred.

"Ha! I thought you had gone and died on me!"

The torso moaned.

"Sorry, what was that?" he asked it.

The half-body pushed up off the ground with its only arm until it was lying on an angle. Tired, bloodshot eyes met his as the pale, drawn, bearded face let out a dry rasp.

"I didn't catch that. You are going to have to speak up Mr Ex, if you want me to hear you."

"Good morning, Mr Chilinski," Mr Ex managed to spit out.

"Morning? Ha! It's late in the afternoon. We are going to have to get you a watch! No, wait. Your watch is supposed to go on your left arm, right?" Mr Chilinski laughed hard at his own joke, his face going red, tears running down his cheeks. "I knew you would make me feel better, Mr Ex. Did you miss me?"

"Sure," he said, dryly.

"Anything happen while I was out?" Mr Chilinski asked, chuckling again.

"Not a lot. I wish you'd leave me something to do when you go away for long stretches. It really gets boring in here."

"Ah. So *I* am supposed to be the one entertaining *you* now, is it?" From his tone Mr Ex knew better than to push him much further.

"No, not at all. Just an occasional book and some light to read it with," he mumbled.

Mr Chilinski grunted. 'We'll see. You'll have to start pulling your weight around here first. Sorry, I didn't mean that literally!"

Mr Ex waited patiently for him to stop laughing. "What would you like me to do?"

"Well, half the reason I keep you here is for the entertainment. So, here I am now. Entertain me!"

"Is the cage really that necessary? I mean, I'm not exactly going anywhere. And while we're talking, some food would be nice."

"Not very entertaiiiiinning ..."

"Okay. What would you like from me?"

"Maybe a joke?"

"Umm. Alright. What do you get when you cross an elephant and a rhino?"

"Heard that one."

"What's the difference between Bitcoin and NASA?"

"Heard that one, too."

"What is the difference between an ATM and a Jewish scuba diver?"

"My mother is Jewish," Mr Chilinski warned.

"Well, I don't know! I probably only know about five jokes. It's not like I have access to the internet, or anything."

"Well then, sing me a song!"

"A song? Are you serious?"

"Do I look serious?" Mr Chilinski asked. He did.

Mr Ex grimaced. He didn't exactly feel like singing, but he knew better than to disobey his captor. He tried to think of a song, any song he could remember. One came to him. He cleared his throat.

When you were here before
Couldn't look you in the eye
You're just like an angel
Your skin makes me cry
You float like a feather
In a beautiful world
I wish I was special
You're so fuckin' special!

His voice began breaking as he tried to hit the higher notes.

But I'm a creep!
I'm a weirdooooo
What the hell am I doin' here?
I don't belong here!

"No, no, no! Not like that! C'mon man. That was horrible! What even was that? You can't tell a joke, can't sing a song. What can you do? You probably aren't even that good in the bedroom, I'm guessing," he said, smirking.

Mr Ex winced. The jab hit hard. He knew he would never know the touch of a woman again. He thought back to all that he had lost. A tear ran down his cheek.

Mr Chilinski threw the remains of the cognac in his face. Mr Ex looked up at him surprised. Despite himself, he sucked what he could from his moustache. He hadn't had anything to drink since he could remember. The alcohol burned his dry, cracked lips.

Mr Chilinski leaned forward.

"I've warned you about crying," he said in a low voice. "Remember, if I grow bored of you there are still things you can lose. That right arm of yours, perhaps?"

"No! Fine. I'll tell you a story then."

"A story? You mean, like a bedtime story?" He asked, a dumb smirk on his face.

"Umm ... sure! But not one for kids. One for adults."

Mr Chilinski undid his cuff links and placed them on his desk. He unbuttoned his collar, refilled his glass and put his feet back on top of the cage.

"You have my attention. Proceed."

Mr Ex took a deep breath and began.

"Once upon a time there was a man named Doug. Now Doug was a very ordinary person. He had a very ordinary childhood. He had an ordinary job, lived in an ordinary house, with his ordinary family. He had ordinary friends, some ordinary hobbies and would take ordinary holidays in the same ordinary places every year."

"This story sounds pretty ordinary," Mr Chilinski complained.

"Be patient, it's going somewhere. Now, Doug had a very ordinary life. Until one day he lost his ordinary job. Someone had realised that paying people in this country was costing more than paying someone else in another country. So Doug was made redundant by his company. Unfortunately for Doug the market was flooded with redundant office workers with the same skill-set as he had. As you probably guessed, Doug's résumé was ordinary."

"Now Doug's wife was a pleasant enough person when she got what she wanted. But, apparently, an unemployed husband was not something that she wanted. So after a few weeks of losing his ordinary job, Doug found that he had lost his ordinary family and ordinary house as well. It wasn't long before his ordinary friends too, made themselves scarce. This made Doug very sad, so one day he found himself standing on the ledge of an ordinary building."

Mr Chilinski's blurry eyes opened wide. He had not heard this story before.

"With one small step Doug fell from a thirty storey building onto his head. Now, this would usually be the end of the tale, but Doug woke up after a little while with the realisation that he wasn't ordinary at all, but he was extraordinary. He stared up at the building astonished. He wiped his head and found that the blood had already dried. He stretched his muscles, twisted his back and checked for broken bones but, besides the initial pain he suffered when he landed, he had no signs of injury. That was when Doug realised he was invincible."

Mr Chilinski closed his eyes. Watching him, Mr Ex continued.

"Doug had no idea what to do with his new-found talent, namely that of not dying. He tested it out just to make sure it wasn't a fluke, grabbing hold of live electrical cables, holding bricks on the bottom of a lake; he even lit a rag hanging out of the gas tank of his car and sat inside until it exploded. After a lot of this ... unpleasantness, we'll call it, he realised two things; One: that he was indeed invincible and, Two: he was now without a car."

Mr Chilinski didn't react. Mr Ex guessed that he must have fallen asleep.

"Go on. I didn't tell you to stop," he said, eyes still closed.

"Right! Sorry. So, Doug decided that he wanted to be a vigilante. You know, like the movies. Except no spandex. No cape. No mask. No catch-phrases. No side-kick. Just an angry unkillable man and his fists.

He walked around the city late at night, looking for a group of guys up to no good to vent his anger on. It didn't take him long to find one. The thing that Doug didn't understand at first was that to be an effective vigilante it helps if you know how to fight. The men in the alley took turns at beating him and, after they tired of that, they took his wallet, watch and phone. Being a vigilante turned out to be an expensive hobby. So he figured he needed to find a job.

So, Doug took an open position at a security company. It seemed like the logical choice. They trained him how to deal with violent people, how to use a night-stick, mace and handcuffs. In his spare time he took self-defence lessons, all that he could attend. He started with boxing, then Muay Thai kick-boxing, but before long he was mixing Kung-fu, wrestling and Krav Maga, broadening his skills. After a couple of years he turned into a pretty decent fighter, too. He could take on two or three people at a time and, because of his drive, found himself winning nearly all of the matches he entered. But Doug never lost his direction. He didn't view fighting as a sport, but an instrument, a tool to be used for a purpose. When he felt that he was ready, he tracked down those same guys in the alleyway, surprisingly they hadn't changed their hang-out spot and their second encounter turned out a lot different to the first. He even managed to get his watch back.

Fuelled with the adrenaline of success, Doug decided that he was going to make a difference. Too old to start any kind of military career, he resolved that he was going to clean up his city and he was going to start from the top. He was going to tackle its organised-crime problem."

Mr Chilinski opened his eyes and smiled, showing his teeth.

"Sounds like a brave man, this 'Doug.'"

"He was, at least he tried to be. He saw a problem and wanted to fix it. Surprisingly, it wasn't hard to track down a crime family. Their restaurants and cafés were notorious, always in the news, but the police gave them a wide berth, not wanting to stir the hive. He became a regular at these places, paying attention to the suits who came and went. Until one day he hit the jackpot. The son of a notorious gangster walked in unexpectedly and ordered a chicken and avocado linguine. Doug couldn't believe his luck."

"After he finished his meal, the gangster left in a black car with some of his henchmen. Doug followed them back to a factory. He thought he had caught them in the act of a crime. But when he forced his way inside he found the factory was empty and was only being used as office space. When I say empty, I'm ignoring the twenty-or-so men he had in there with him. Having blown his cover, all Doug could do was fight. And fight he did. Using his training and the few weapons he had on him, he punched, kicked, stabbed and used men as shields as he took them down, one by one. He must have put at least half of them in hospital before he started losing steam."

"Eight."

"Sorry?"

"You put eight of my men in hospital."

"Right. Anyway, this is my story. May I continue?"

"Of course! Sorry for interrupting," he said, sarcastically.

"So, after he had taken down at least twelve of the men, he began to tire. And, despite being invincible, the pain from the bullets and blades became unbearable. He realised that yet again he had underestimated his opponent. Held against the ground with his hands tied behind his back, the last thing he saw that night was a metal baseball bat being dragged on the floor towards him." He paused. "When he woke up ... darkness."

Mr Chilinski smiled. He was enjoying the story. Mr Ex could see the cold cruelty behind his eyes.

"So what happened next?"

"Well, the men had realised after a few attempts that Doug was in-executable. So the crime-boss decided on a cruel and unique punishment for the intruder. He had his men concrete him into his office floor, leaving one hand free for him to feed himself. He then bolted a cage over the top of his prisoner, to give the impression of an animal, a freak. From then on, everytime he had a meeting with new partners or rival gangs he would remove the cage cover, showing them his prize. All men that entered his office could never forget what they saw and they would agree to most anything he asked for, their uneasy eyes constantly returning to his captive. It was a warning to anyone that would dare oppose him; there are worse punishments than death.”

“Correct!” Mr Chilinski agreed. Putting his shoes back on, he stood up and stretched. “That was a really good story! I especially enjoyed the ending. This ‘Doug’ character thought he had lost everything. Until he found out he had yet more to lose. He still had his health. He still had his freedom.”

“He still had his name,” Mr Ex said, emotion creeping into his voice.

“Anyway,” Mr Chilinski said abruptly, walking to the door and putting his jacket on, “We have a big day of work tomorrow and I need to get home for some rest. I will see you tomorrow!”

“Goodnight Mr Chilinski.”

“Goodnight Mr Example.”

With a soft click, the room returned to darkness.

15 The Adventures of Edmund *by Jeremy Picknell*

Author's note: Can an inanimate object be a hero? The author thought he would start writing and find out ...

*

The chariot raced past at a thunderous pace, shaking the ground and throwing dust into the air. This time, the iron rim of the wheel missed Edmund by just inches. But he wasn't scared. Instead he was overcome with awe; at the horses, the crack of the whip and the charioteer's bronze helmet with its bright red plume of feathers. He ached to be on that chariot so much that he would have burst into tears, had he been able to.

Gradually the dust settled on Edmund and his friends. They thought he was mad. Not only because they were terrified of being run over, but because he had no business dreaming of charioteers, horses or stadiums. No business either dreaming of flying like a bird, or falling in love, which he had once confided. Because, simply put, Edmund was a stone. Not a particularly large one, below average if the truth was to be told. His shape was nothing grand either, nor round and smooth like a beach pebble, but jagged in a lopsided way, drawing speculation from others about him being a mistake.

Edmund found stones a conservative lot. They couldn't run away from the numerous dangers they faced, such as being crushed by a chariot, placed inside a boy's slingshot, or imprisoned inside concrete. So, they had learned over thousands of years since homo sapiens came, to run away deep inside themselves, drawing their energy inward for protection. But Edmund wasn't like that. He was interested in the world. His aching for experience pulled his consciousness right to the edge of all of his odd shaped surfaces. Once, when his longing had pressed particularly hard against these walls, he felt, in fact

82

he was sure, that he had actually moved a fraction along the ground. Just the tiniest of fractions, but movement nonetheless.

"Ridiculous," had said the elder Gareth. "It would have been a tremor in the Earth that moved you, or subterranean water unsettling the dirt underneath."

"Then why didn't it move you too?" argued Edmund.

"Because I'm bigger, and… I have gravitas."

Again, the chariot approached. Edmund sensed the stones around him retreating further inside themselves, until their beings were as tiny as pinheads. But he wanted a closer look at the charioteer's helmet, at its vibrant red feathers fluttering in the wind. As the chariot turned into the straight, Edmund realized that the two horses were charging straight at him, the barrelling rim of a wheel looming larger and larger. Edmund braced himself for the hit.

As the horses leapt over him, a hoof pounded the tip of his lopsided protrusion into the dirt, catapulting him into the air with a chaotic spin. The ground and sky whizzed around him in a whirl of confusion. Eventually he stopped spinning. Not abruptly, like hitting a brick wall, but with a soft landing. Miraculously, Edmund found that he was lodged in the gap between the charioteer's breastplate strap and his tunic.

Nestled there snuggly, Edmund took in his surrounds; the sweaty, determined face of the charioteer, his bronze helmet with its nose and cheek guards and further up, to Edmund's delight, the column of red feathers. Edmund stared, transfixed. They didn't seem to be just blowing aimlessly in the wind, but dancing together exuberantly, freely, happily. So unlike stones. Edmund made up his mind there and then, he was going to be like them.

Edmund spent a breezy, glorious afternoon with the feathers. He could feel almost a soul connection with them and he was sure that they bent down towards him a number of times in order to include him. Eventually the charioteer pulled up and handed the reins over to a servant. They went through an elaborate archway, down a maze of stone passageways and into a bedchamber. The charioteer pulled off his helmet and placed it carefully on top of an oak bedside table. Reaching for his breast plate strap, he noticed Edmund nestled there. He clasped him between his thumb and finger and pulled him out from his cosy nook. Edmund saw a pair of large, brown eyes studying him curiously, before being tossed onto the bedside table and into the side of the helmet with a clang. The charioteer pulled off his tunic, spread eagled himself across the bed and relaxed with a deep sigh.

Above him, Edmund's new friends hung limply from the helmet. Looking around, he was surprised to discover right next to him a gold ring, inset with a red garnet stone. Not the vibrant, playful red of his new friends, but a deep red, both rich and elegant. The garnet's surface was decorated with perfectly cut triangles, which reflected light at all angles, creating a symphony of red and black shapes. Edmund gazed through the middle circle of triangles. The red seemed to go on forever, as if he was looking into eternity. He had never imagined before how beautiful a stone could be.

His whole awareness now attuned to the garnet, Edmund sensed that there was a presence inside. A 'she'. Looking closer, he saw a tiny spark of light, one moment in one part of the garnet, the next moment in another. Finally, the spark came close to the surface, noticed him and retreated inside. Edmund felt a tingling through the whole of his stone. Earnestly he examined every part of the garnet, including the corner of every triangle, but couldn't find the spark anywhere. At least for now, she was gone.

Edmund had nothing else to do, but to wait and watch. Inexplicably, the charioteer raised his hands in the air, brought them together in a single, loud clap and rolled on to his stomach. Edmund focused back on the garnet. Deep inside, he thought he saw the faintest of sparks. Then again, but this time a little closer. The third time it was inside a triangle on the far left of the stone and then, getting closer now, on the right side. He had the feeling that the spark was checking him out from different angles. He waited in anticipation for another showing, but it didn't come. Eventually he concluded she must have lost interest, perhaps finding his protrusion off-putting.

Edmund was so focussed on the garnet, that he got a shock when a ceramic bowl was placed on the other side of him. With one smooth, flowing movement, a small, delicate hand entered the bowl and re-emerged, fingers dripping with oil. A woman with flowing, jet-black hair and skimpy, exotic attire, straddled the charioteer. She began gliding her hands up and down his back.

"Aaah," sighed the charioteer.

The woman chuckled playfully in response. Edmund didn't know what to make of this and turned his attention back to the garnet.

To his surprise, 'she' was now a pinpoint of light observing him right at the surface of the garnet. No longer a momentary spark, but a constant presence. Edmund knew he should say something but couldn't think what.

"I got a ride here on the chariot," he blurted out, realizing straight away how stupid it sounded.

The light at first didn't seem to respond, then transformed into a shape, reminiscent of a smile. Edmund's confidence grew.

Laughter and giggling came from the direction of the bed.

The light changed back into a circle. They looked at each other awkwardly.

"What's it like being made into a ring?"

Edmund could tell it was the wrong question when the light tried changing into a number of shapes without settling on any, before giving up the attempt.

The laughter behind Edmund was turning into all sorts of grunts and gasps. He tried to ignore them, fearing that the light might lose interest and disappear again inside her garnet. He realized he needed to be bold.

"I love your triangles," he said, as smoothly as he could.

Edmund watched anxiously as the light went through various contortions, making him wonder if he had blown it. Finally, she morphed into a shape of a heart. He was so happy, he wanted to break into a dance, like one of his feather friends would have done.

"I'm Edmund, by the way."

She morphed into a star, then somehow made it pulsate.

"Stella? Your name is Stella!"

Again, she morphed into a smile, then changed back into her heart shape. From the bed came the sound of snoring. It didn't bother Edmund, he was content just gazing at Stella.

The delicate hand appeared at the bowl again, picked it up, held it in the air for a moment, and then put it back down. Instead, the hand hovered over the ring. All of a sudden, it swooped and snatched it up with finger and thumb.

"Stella!" shouted Edmund.

He just managed to catch a flicker of her as she sparked around inside the garnet in a panic, before disappearing down the crevice of the woman's blouse.

"Stella!"

The woman tiptoed out the room.

"Don't worry, I'll rescue you!" cried out Edmund.

But he had no idea how he would do this. Devastated and powerless to do anything, he retreated inside himself. On the bed, the charioteer snored.

It felt cold, deep inside the stone. Not so much the temperature, Edmund was used to that. But cold in a lifeless, staid, sort of way. He tried to imagine hiding in there forever. There were benefits, he began to realize. Even if there was an earthquake or tsunami outside, he could still remain untroubled, sober, dignified. Only a 'hot rocks sauna' type scenario could unduly affect him. But what about Stella and seeing her dancing spark again? "No," said Edmund to himself. "The chance of that is about as poor as seeing old Gareth cheery." Time to get serious and mind his own business like the rest of the stones.

There was a sudden jolt and shaking of the table, making Edmund move a fraction along its surface. For a moment he wondered what it was. "Ha! I don't need to worry about things like that anymore," he told himself.

He went back to practising his new, stuffy disposition. He heard snoring and only then realised that the charioteer must have stirred in his sleep.

Again, the table jolted and the snoring stopped. Could it be something to do with Stella? He couldn't resist taking a look and began the journey through his many layers of grey until he reached the surface. Looking down, he could see that the cause of the disturbance was the charioteer bumping his leg against the side-table in his sleep. With eyes still closed, the charioteer yawned, as if about to wake up. Edmund became hopeful. Maybe if he noticed his ring was missing, there would still be time for him to catch the masseuse before she got too far away. But to Edmund's dismay, he started snoring again.

"I wish I wasn't a stone!" cried out Edmund, as if any other object around him could hear. He looked up at the bright red feathers, but they hung as powerless as he from the helmet. Peering down over the side of the table, he saw the charioteer's knee directly below. He thought that if he could only get himself to move again and topple off the edge on to the charioteer, he may be able to wake him up. He remembered Gareth ridiculing him for thinking he could move. "Well Gareth. You know what you can do with your gravitas!"

Edmund knew it was going to be tough moving himself a full inch to get to the edge when last time he had only moved a fraction of that. He concentrated on evoking the same feeling that had moved him before and projected it forwards, towards the table-edge. Edmund thought of the chariot rushing past; the feathers dancing freely in the wind, their bright red colour deliciously offset by the blue sky behind them. How he longed to be like them. But when he checked, he hadn't even moved a hair width along the table.

This time Edmund imagined he was the charioteer himself, feeling the wind rushing into his face and on through the gap between cheek and helmet, looking down at the horses as he flicked the whip, seeing the ground rush by beneath their hooves. It was like he was really there. But again, no movement.

He wondered if Gareth was right after all. That it was just his imagination that made him think he had moved last time. Then he thought of Stella and realized his mistake. The reason he wasn't moving, was that it was *her* he most wanted now, not the wind, dancing feathers or chariot rides.

This time he concentrated on when he had met Stella; the deep red of her garnet, her spark appearing here and there in her triangles, then finally appearing as a spot of light in front of him.

Edmund checked the distance. Finally, he had moved a bit, but only a quarter of the way. Above him the feathers started shivering ever so slightly in a breeze too slight for him to feel. Or were they fluttering for him? Urging him on?

Edmund concentrated like he never had before. He remembered his nervousness as Stella was morphing shape and then his relief when she turned into a smile. And then his sheer joy when she broke into a shape of a heart. How he longed to see her again …

Suddenly Edmund felt himself falling. A split second later his protrusion hit the inside of the charioteer's knee.

The charioteer stopped snoring and sat up. Rubbing his knee, he saw Edmund on the floor below him and picked him up. He eyed him as he held him between thumb and finger, recognized him, then looked confused over at the bedside table. His face changed to rage. He dropped Edmund back on the floor.

"Cornelia!" he shouted as he barged out of the room.

Edmund lay on the slate floor, listening to sounds of shouting spread outside like an infectious disease.

"Idiot," said the piece of slate underneath him. "Look what you've done now!"

"Shut up!" said Edmund, irritated. "Just go back to being trodden on!"

All of the other pieces of slate started calling Edmund names in support of their colleague, but he paid them no more attention. He was too busy listening for signs of Stella being found.

Finally, Edmund heard footsteps and moments later, the charioteer entered, knelt down beside the bed and pulled out a jewellery box from underneath. To Edmund's relief he produced Stella from inside his tunic, but then promptly put her in the box and snapped the lid shut. As he adjusted his position to push the box back under the bed, he bumped his hand on Edmund.

"Umm," said the charioteer, picking Edmund up and eyeing him curiously. "Perhaps you are a lucky stone." He opened the lid again and put him inside as well.

When Edmund told Stella the whole story, including how he had managed to alert the charioteer, she turned into a shape of a tear, dropped to a splash, then magically became a heart, all in one smooth motion. From then on, they were forever bonded.

Although they had many happy times together, Stella occasionally had to go away for long periods on campaigns and Edmund, left behind in the darkness, would worry that the charioteer would get killed in battle and Stella be taken off by a Gaul or Visigoth. But she always came back and there, in the dark of the box with no other light, she sparkled even brighter, playing hide and seek in her triangles, making hearts for Edmund and other shapes that are best not mentioned. Edmund enjoyed her shows and perhaps a little mischievously, the fact that the charioteer was oblivious to the goings-on inside his jewellery box. Oblivious also, like every other human, to the simple fact that the light which can be seen in a gemstone, or in any other stone for that matter, isn't just a reflection of light from outside, but a spark from deep within its being.

16 The Role Model *by Kerry Sharp*

Author's note: Childhood influences lead to strange places.

*

Maybe it was the click of the door which woke him up or even the Jasmin perfume of the intruder, but his eyes flew open to see a Goddess standing before his bed. An overcoat fell and pooled at her feet.

As if responding to a silent appeal the clouds cleared, fine-spun moonbeams caressed her, their threads of lights played with her femininity. They were not eager and didn't deign to show her in colour but subtly in monochrome. The exquisite play of light and shadow displayed her deliciously, attenuating her curves revealing a sexual woman in in a way that spot lights would have failed to achieve.

He heard a swish of silk as her gossamer gown joined the coat. NOW the moonbeams were eager. Unimpeded by clothing, the light frolicked happy to fondle her curves to dive and gambol in her valleys. She would have been beautiful even if the light didn't love her. As she moved towards his bed, shadow and light fought in a dance of adulation. His earlier thought of Goddess didn't cut it, he toyed with Angel but her lascivious smile promised a paradise that had nothing to do with heaven.

The bed rocked as she sat and pulled the sheets off him. Thoughts of adjectives failed, had he been cognisant he would have realised where the blood-flow necessary for thought had migrated.

'Mm-mm!' she purred.

Her hand caressed his bare body. She mounted him and grasped the only part of his body that was not confused, she directed it towards her warmth. Her eyebrow raised in question,

91

he nodded.

He was more inflamed by her libidinous smile than her invading warmth. He would have thought it impossible for anything to be more provoking than the physical. But the promise in her prurient smile would have roused him, even had he been swimming in an Arctic pool.

Her smile slipped from libidinous to wanton yet despite her obvious arousal she dawdled as if testing his resolve to continue. The only resolve he could find had nothing to do with stopping her, he lifted his hands to her hips and echoed her movements. Nodding she increased her pace as if acknowledging he was now complicit in the action.

He took her in, his focus had funnelled, she was intoxicating. All of her body moved, a symphony in sympathy. Her breasts rocked in counterpoint to her body as she undulated, her nipples shouted her arousal.

Observing his gaze, she said, 'Good boy, you like my breasts?'

She lifted his hands from her hips they willingly followed to cup her. Her perky orbs fitted his hands to perfection. She coached his hands to pleasure her.

The moonlight that adored her enfolded him in its embrace; it loved the two humans who were revelling in the oldest dance. Maybe it was a waltz; slow and elegant, or a Cha Cha; vibrant and cheeky but whatever the dance after two circuits of the floor the conclusion was fast and inevitable.

He watched her left eye twitch, her stomach muscles flutter, as her velvet sleeve pulsed her pleasure in a Morse code which his body understood, he joined her. They screamed their pleasure in harmony. A scouring flame scorched them, coursing through their bodies tripping nerve endings and pleasure centres to feed their joy.

A chemical cocktail of neurohormones, oxytocin, endorphins and prolactin flooded their brains. The high was too high, they slumped together boneless. Savouring lingering pleasure, shared warmth and gentle caresses, they slept.

Alex awoke feeling serene but sad, he focused to account for the strange feelings. He was sad because he was alone. Was it real?

The dampness in the bed gave the impossible event credence, yet the hydraulics could have been a solo enterprise. Then the unmistakable smell of aroused woman and the lingering trace of perfume convinced him his memory, although surreal, was true.

'Christ, no one will believe me,' he said to the room. Then he realised the moment was too intimate for sharing, it was a gift of great value, a memory to take to theHe had intended to shower, but he now understood why his niece refused to wash the hand that touched Justin Bieber. He found fresh clothes to avoid diluting her essence.

Alex was gathering his reports preparing for the tribunal when an envelope appeared under his door. More interested in the postie than post he rushed to the door and stepped into an empty corridor.

'They were bloody fast!' he mumbled to himself as he knelt and picked up the missive and pressed it to his nose. It disappointed him it didn't smell of Jasmine.

He was representing the Shire; he was the Mayor of Koojahvale, the town most affected by the proposed development. His friends said if he could not quash the proposal, he would kill the antagonists. It was a joke, but it reflected the strength of his opposition, the development would destroy his town whose only sin was being too close to the city.

He opened and scanned the documents in his hands. Southern Star Global now owned the project. They were no longer fighting Dodge Constructions or Dodgy Con as the opponents of the project insisted on calling them. He scanned the memorandum finding a slew of keywords; sympathetic development, enhanced agrarian synergy, collegiate planning, partnership in amenity, it was just corporate speak, Southern Star would screw them without a smile.

The tribunal was as he expected corporate double speak from those who wanted to do, and emotive tangle talk from those that didn't. He was tiring of hearing two minutes of value spread over ten minutes of speech when the room stirred.

'No wonder she's doubled the value of Southern Star looking like that.' His neighbour mumbled.

He thought it was an "old man" comment, sure she looked nice but businessmen were too canny to be swayed by a trim figure or gentle ways. She manoeuvred almost diffidently to a seat towards the back, every eye followed her. She at least achieved something useful the speaker stopped pontificating until she sat. When seated she gave a subtle bow of acknowledgement to the massed eyes. After that display he decided that HE was too canny to be influenced.

The speaker resumed, his monotone had surrendered to interest or more accurately he was trying to interest a particular audience member. Alex looked at his watch twenty minutes till coffee. For him the refreshment table was the most interesting thing in the room.

Alex sighed, not only was the coffee excellent, but he'd snagged a glazed doughnut and a Danish as a dunker. He zigged and zagged around the crowd to a quiet corner; he didn't want a careless elbow to interrupt dunking.

'Will you help me save your part of paradise?' He heard behind him.

Turning, he saw the woman of the moment and sensed the aggression of the men she had ignored to reach him.

'Sorry, I'm Gina North,' she said, offering her hand.

'Alex McKee,' he took it.

'Don't let me stop you from dunking.'

'You won't,' he said defensively, how did she know he was about to dunk?

She looked at him expectantly; he was still wondering about the dunking.

'Paradise,' she prompted.

'Ms North, I don't trust you. Corporate speak overwhelmed English in your explanatory document. I believe Southern Star will screw us without even smiling.'

She shook her head, offended. Then her creased forehead surrendered to a cheeky grin.

'You smell nice!'

He blushed, he knew the genesis of his perfume; he hoped she didn't. Her crinkled eyes and the mischief in her grin showed he could hope all he liked, she knew.

'Yes, it's a new male perfume,' he bluffed. 'I don't know what it's called.'

'Unobtainium, maybe?'

Her grin morphed into a monster smile, which licked his face as she turned away to grace someone else with her presence.

She spun back, 'I smiled,' she added before striding back to her seat.

Christ, his midnight visitor was Gina North. He thought she'd seemed familiar but Gina North was a total stranger, Why?

The facilitator who was shouting over the still boisterous crowd interrupted his thoughts.

'Attention ... Attention ... Southern Star is the new developer and to present their perspective is Ms North. Ladies and Gentlemen Gina North!'

He held up his hand like a Ring Master as she weaved through the chairs to the podium. The room fell into an attentive hush as all eyes followed her slalom.

After the opening address Gina looked at Alex.

'I hope to melt the heart of my sternest enemy,' she held his eye, 'but ONLY through the strength of this proposal.'

Her eyes left him to sweep the room to draw others, through emotion, to her viewpoint.

'I don't want sycophants! I want people who identify with Southern Star's objectives. I have been told by a witness to this tribunal that Southern Star will screw you without even a smile. I'll come back to that later.'

Her eyes settled fleetingly on Alex again. There was a subtext to her words. If she didn't visit his room to influence him, then why did she? Alex was having trouble concentrating, his head was spinning. Every time he reined his thoughts to focus on the speaker he saw moonbeams and her body, but it didn't fit. He knew she was panchromatic even though he'd only seen shadows play with her but now she seemed veiled. Shiny rather than colourful, showy rather than vibrant, chromed rather than lustred.

'What the ...' he grumbled to himself. 'Whatever she proposes, I will oppose-'

'Can you be quiet I'm listening ... or trying to!'

Alex glared at his neighbour, it wasn't listening the old bugger wanted to do. His anger settled his brain, he found focus. When the laughter subsided, he framed her words not her body.

'Dodgy Con ... ops sorry, Dodge Constructions were optimistic in their estimates of density and underestimated local sentiment. Southern Star's research convinced Dodgy Con their proposal at this tribunal would fail. We offered them an alternative which they took. I hope you all received your envelops under your doors this morning?'

There were general murmurings of consent.

'The same delegate also told me that although the document comprised words, none of them were in English-'

Laughter interrupted, she held up her hands; the merriment stilled.

'And I agree. The document should have said we love the area and we want to do the right thing.'

The applause was generous; she had won most of the delegates but without Alex she would not win the day. He was representing the town and the Shire. They had changed the planning overlay, at the next Council meeting they would adopt it, it doomed her project. He couldn't help sharing his smug grin. Gina took a big breath and pulled her shoulders back, a fight it would be then. She held up her hand, again the room stilled.

'Back to an earlier point, Southern Star never screws people without a smile,' her eyes found Alex again, 'we always smile, because we always win. Let me tell you why.'

There was nothing coy about the glare she focused on Alex.

'We always win because Southern Star Global has the cheapest financing cost of any Australian developer. A loss in Hicks Town to many would not be costly, to us it would be. Anything that erodes our investors' confidence would increase the cost base of ALL our projects.'

She scanned the crowd and caught the eye of each individual.

'Once we put our imprimatur on a project, that project WILL go ahead.'

The mood had changed, no one saw a pretty girl but a powerful woman. The power and the sway she had on the delegates impressed Alex, but he was no pushover. He raised his hand.

'Yes, Mayor Alex McKee, you have a question?'

'Yes, Ms North I do.'

'Before you ask your question Mayor McKee, you may like to know the State Government have vetoed any change to the planning overlay.'

Alex sucked in a breath, he didn't know but he didn't doubt her; she continued.

'Alex, will you work with me, please?'

The words sounded ordinary to everyone else's ears but the pleading smile which accompanied them shouted to Alex. He watched the play of emotion on her face.

'Yes, I will,' he said.

Alex looked around, he expected backlash from the "don't want" crowd but they all smiled at him.

After the breakthrough the tribunal meandered through the motions and ticked all the tribunal boxes while the delegates snored, lunch couldn't come soon enough.

Alex took his sausage rolls to a quiet corner and gave them the attention they deserved, he looked up when the hub-hub in the room stilled. Gina walked towards him in full colour.

'Thank you for your support Unclex, it wasn't why I visited you. I've wanted to do that for years.'

'Georgina ... Georgie Dillon?'

She kissed his cheek.

'Why Gina?' he stuttered more for something to say while his brain re-booted.

'Gina is a better name for a rich widow. Gina is also the CEO construct.'

He pulled her into a hug. She was one of his niece's coterie of friends, a solid group of five. They called him Unclex, claiming it was better than Uncle Lex.

'I'm sorry I missed Helen's funeral, my husband chose that day to die.'

'I'm sorry too Georgie.'

She smiled at the name. The silence stretched.

'Why me Georgie, I thought you would have forgotten me. Plus, you could have anyone?'

She hugged him this time; it reminded her of earlier hugs he'd shared with the group of silly girls. Who could only express their desire by repeatedly prodding him with their pubescent breasts. But he'd ignored their immature advances and instead treated them like adults.

'Unclex I've thought about you almost every night, guess what I've called my vibrator?'

'Lex?' he asked laughing.

'No, Unclex, like the rest of the girls.'

His eyes flew open.

'Your niece too is a strong, sensual woman.'

'Christ, Georgie don't tell her.'

'She already knows, they all do.'

'But ... but ... why?'

She took pity on him.

'We loved Helen as much as you otherwise we would have all visited you carnally. But Unclex the wait was worth it.'

She caressed his cheek.

'All five of us married well, lasting relationships with love. That's not a surprise, you were the hurdle other men had to jump. From all five of us, thank you!'

She walked away, the noise in the room restarted. She threw a parting comment over her shoulder. 'Unclex, they'll all visit, lock your door if you find that unpleasant.'

Her colours faded, she was once again a stranger. Maybe she stepped back behind the corporate cloud where automatons were currency and real people treacled the works?

17 Suspicious Minds *by Sohom Das*

Author's note: What happens when an unwelcome stranger enters the close-knit cliquey world of Elvis impersonators?

*

In his striped black and white prison fatigues, looking not unlike an agitated zebra, Elvis paced as best he could, restricted by the dimensions of the cramped backstage dressing room. The glistening metal chain around his ankle, trailed him, tinkling against the floor. The odour of sweat mingled with the stale despair of decades of under-appreciated entertainers. The walls were adorned with dozens of ancient yellowing photographs of performers who had the misfortune of trudging through this venue. Their poses were all remarkably similar; fingers pointed at the camera and plastered-on smiles, failing to camouflage weary eyes. A museum of desperation.

Elvis cursed under his breath and leapt up on to a stool. The chain followed him loyally, clanging. With a grunt, he forced open a tiny window in the corner of the room above a photo of an eighties game-show host he vaguely recognised. A window that paradoxically seemed to bring darkness into the already dim, dungeon of a room. He dug out a packet of cigarettes and threw one into his mouth.

"Come on. You know you can't smoke in here."

Elvis yelped. The stool wobbled. He hadn't even noticed the tubby man on the sofa, despite his conspicuous white jumpsuit. The man pulled off his huge black quiffed wig and winced as he stripped off his furry sideburns. Massaging his bald head, he let out a sigh which stretched into a groan.

"James, Elvis is not Indian," Elvis barked back. He flicked at his plastic lighter, which nonchalantly spat out the occasional spark.

101

"Well, maybe it's good to have a bit of diversity for once. With Black Lives Matter shenanigans and all that. The world is sensitive right now."

"Elvis. Is. *Not.* Indian." Elvis' teeth clenched as if barely containing the venom inside, as he shook his lighter ferociously, before flinging it against the wall. It bounced back and hit him on the chin. The eighties game-show host's grin mocked him through the frame.

"Elvis *was* not Indian, Elvis. *Was.* You need to stop talking about him in the present. It's not healthy."

The tiny door creaked open and a lanky, ghostly-pale man with a straggly beard ducked through it. His costume was very similar to James'. He surveyed the scene dark, behind glittery glasses. "Is the cry-baby spitting out his dummy?" he scoffed, before taking a swig from a can of Fosters.

"Take it easy Dewie. He's not in a good mood," James muttered.

Elvis turned around carefully, poised on his stool, and marvelled at the two men. One obese, one emaciated. One bald, one hirsute. Both in white jumpsuits, with red lapels and golden tassels on their shoulders. He shook his head slowly. "Look at you two. You're like opposite ends of an eating disorder."

James emitted a nervous chuckle.

"It's not funny!" screamed Elvis. The stool creaked. "You're bloody amateurs. The King doesn't have a beard, Dewie. And going on stage in the same bloody outfits! You couldn't have checked, beforehand?"

"Mine's got a cape," James mumbled.

"Oh, get off your high horse," Dewie said, just as Elvis climbed down from the stool. "It's just a bit of fun." He lifted the can and gulped several long swigs.

"Fun?" Elvis' hands contracted into fists. "Do you want the

Annual Norwich Elvis Impersonation Contest to turn into some kind of novelty? Do you want some… random man in a tacky party outfit to bring shame upon the King? Massacring one of his songs to a bunch of baying imbeciles?"

The question was rhetorical, yet still, the lack of response filled Elvis with wrath. The room seemed to shrink. "I can't believe you guys aren't angrier!" He pulled out his pack of cigarettes, then remembering that his lighter didn't work, tossed them onto the table. "When *real* dedicated fans of the King, people devoted to him, to this craft, *we* just get overlooked."

The buzzing strip-light above flickered, as if concurring. Performers grinned inanely from the walls, unphased.

"Oh I get it," said Dewie. "You're miffed because a brown man won."

"Did he put the hours in? Does he have a bloody internet webby page… thingy? Does he drive three hours to Hull and back every month for a show?"

"Oh, and you just assume you should have won, Elvis? Your arrogance is astounding."

"I would have beaten *you!* With your second-rate rendition of Suspicious Minds and white jumpsuit. How unoriginal. My outfit is *official* Jailhouse Rock prison fatigues." He shuffled his feet and the chain clunked with a heavy authenticity. I did a lesser-known song for *true* Elvis fans. Not those ruddy buffoons!" Elvis ran his fingers through his thickly-gelled hair. "Besides, I owe him," he whispered.

"Owe who?"

Elvis looked up and snarled.

Dewie's opened his mouth. His brow furrowed above his dark glasses, but his face was pacified by James' pleading eyes. He sighed, and grabbed another can of Fosters from behind a bin. Elvis' stare stalked him across the room, though lingered on the beer. It looked so very tempting. But he would not slip up. Not again.

Elvis leapt forward and knocked the can out of Dewie's hand, onto the ancient cupboard. His face had turned a darker shade of crimson, creasing up, around his remarkably inert eyebrows. He had instinctively taken on his stage stance, with his pelvis jutting forward and his legs splayed out. One hand went to his hip, as the other threw a finger in Dewie's face. "You don't even *look* like the King. You're two feet too tall and have you seen your skin? You look like you *died* six months ago."

"My skin's too light, and the winner's skin's too dark? Can't you at least be a consistent racist?"

"How dare you!" Elvis' quiff quivered, as if itself outraged. "I'm not a racist. Some of my friends…" His top lip curled microscopically. "…Some of my favourite takeaways are… You're trying to confuse me! I voted against Brexit."

"Look mate, you're taking this far too seriously," Dewie said, rescuing his fallen can, as it haemorrhaged beer.

"Yeah," said James reticently, as if unsure if the others were even still aware of his presence. "There are plenty of other competitions."

"I meant this *whole* thing," said Dewie. "Your life. Changing your name to Elvis. That weird shrine you've got in your living room, that creepy enormous tattoo. And don't think we haven't noticed the botox around your forehead. It's too much, mate. I know you've managed to quit … to get over your …" He slowly moved the beer can behind him. "And that's admiral. But, maybe you've got an addictive personality. Just replacing one vice with another."

Elvis kicked off one shoe. The other one did not cooperate.

"We liked you when you were Barry, mate. Barry was far

more… stable."

Elvis shook his leg vigorously, rattling his chain, but the obstinate shoe remained. He limped closer to Dewie until their nose and chin were almost touching. "When you met me five years ago on the Norwich Elvis circuit you were *nothing! I* took you under my wing. *I* told you about all the gigs. Showed you how to spread out the hits, to keep up the momentum of your set. *Me!*"

Dewie leant backwards and took and awkward sip of his beer. His legs were planted in defiance, but his upper body betrayed fear. "Elvis, I don't want to fight. I just think it's better, healthier, if this isn't your… everything."

As Elvis stared into Dewie's dark shades, he found himself thrust back, inside a flashback of the incident, a month ago. An overwhelming disgrace churned inside him. From his bones. *How could I have slipped up?* He tasted it again. The harsh whisky, deep in the back of his throat. He remembered the blood dripping, meandering down the side of his hand. Shame boiled and fermented into rage. *How could I have even considered turning my back on the King?*

The cramped room shrunk and shrunk and dissolved into oblivion. All he knew was that memory. That harsh whisky. All he saw was glass shards across over the floor. Pieces of the King's face smiling, pouting. Infuriatingly nonchalant. Pieces from within a multitude of ripped photos, strewn across the bedroom, tinged with pink smudges of blood and remorse. And his one true prized possession, an actual autographed photo of the King, which cost him five grand and his marriage, torn and tattered, all over his bed.

The slice of pain that shot through Elvis' scalp pulled him out of his trance. Only then, did he realise James was yanking back on his heavily gelled quiff. Only then, did he find himself lying on top of Dewie, watching his own hands gripping his friends' throat. Only then, was Elvis aware of the demons inside of him, that must have usurped his body.

He heard a gargling noise, a soft whimpering and a rumbling growl and it took several moments to decipher which noise originated from which man. He clambered to his feet and smelled his own lemon fresh Brylcream, smudged across his face by James' fingers, during the struggle. *Reassuringly citrus*, the aptly named flavour. Elvis needed a cigarette.

Dewie stood up. His face was rosy, scratched and terrified. His wig had turned 90 degrees and its quiff protruded, perpendicularly. Elvis looked down at his hands. They felt alien. Borrowed He was holding a clump of gold tassels from Dewie's shoulder.

Elvis wanted to apologise, but all the words he could conjure up felt ludicrous. He allowed James to push him out of the door.

Elvis shuffled through the long corridor around the back of the stage. He heard the cacophony of the crowd. He usually made efforts to mingle with them after the show. Give out the odd autograph. Ostensibly for the fans, but in reality to nourish his withered ego. But not now. He heard Tom Jones' voice crooning that it was not unusual. He heard chatter, laughter and glasses clinking. They were not true fans of the King, and he hated every single one of them.

Before the incident, a month ago, before the guilt, and the overwhelming shame, Elvis had actually been having a good day. He had won twenty pounds on a scratch-card. His 'best of' compilation video had surpassed a hundred views, finally.

And he had even been enjoying the gig that night. Maybe it was his shades or the low lighting. Or maybe it was just the shadow that his ego had cast. But he had mis-read the facial expressions of the crowd. All he saw was two-hundred or so grins. All was good.

He might have expected it from a stag-do. He was profoundly aware of the debauchery and the lack of dignity they brought. Only literal starvation would make him even consider them. Or worse, that hen-do four years ago, when he had been asked to do unspeakable things, just because the stripper hadn't shown up. But a wedding! And he had said, he had emphasised, *three times* when he had the initial conversation with the bride-to-be over the phone, that he was *not* a novelty act. He played for true fans of the King. He had calculated that three times would be the maximum to make his point, and not come across as weird. And three times she had reassured him.

Elvis wondered if she had intentionally lied to him, as he waited impotently at the side of the stage. He stared into those deceitful smiles, moments after the Best Man had pushed him to the side, grabbed the microphone off him and bullied the Groom to come on stage to sing. The crowd had roared. Much louder than they did for Elvis' own meticulously choreographed entrance. *Pushed* and *grabbed*. Not requested. Not agreed. Not courteous. During that initial phone conversation with the bride-to-be, Elvis had specifically offered to allow either her or the Groom to do a duet with him. But it would need to be organised, practiced. Respectful to the King. Not just ad hoc. Not like this. With the Groom crucifying 'Love Me Tender'. With those two-hundred or so grins, that had now lost their disguises. All treacherous and deceitful.

On the lengthy drizzly car journey home, the words circles around, in his head. An intrusive mantra. Not a novelty. *Not* a novelty. *NOT* a novelty. Three times, he had made it clear to her. And a thousand times before her, to all of those customers, over the years. Did *any* of them listen? Did they even care?

Elvis recalled the car journey and had vague images of later waking up with a razor next to him and two bottles of whisky. There were some memories in between but they felt alien. Borrowed. He could not remember his synapses firing, making the decision to betray him. And only six days away from achieving five years of sobriety. And now he would never forget the awkward telephone call to his sponsor the next morning. The disappointment she had tried to secrete, but was nonetheless deafening to Elvis.

He had only a vague recollection of screaming at the King. At his smug chiselled, handsome face and those eyes. Nonchalant. All treacherous and dreamy. Only wisps of punching the walls and smashing so many of the photographs. Of yanking open his bedroom cupboard door, to his secret shrine. Not the one in the living room, for visitors. But the hidden one, for his one truly valued possession. The autographed photo. He held only a dream-like array of sequences of him ripping open his shirt, and staring at his tattoo of the King across his chest. How could he have carried it for twelve years and only now just noticed that it was so hideous?

He remembered picking up his blade with a trembling hand and he remembered vowing to get rid of the inked monstrosity. He had intended to use whisky as an anaesthetic. But, it knocked him unconscious. Praise the King.

The second he stepped outside into the alleyway, Elvis remembered that he had left his cigarettes in the dressing room. He pictured the eighties talk-show host's grinning face and cursed. He looked up and saw him. The Indian Elvis. He was smoking with a couple of friends, in his red jumpsuit. Up close, Elvis immediately recognised the cheap polyester and tacky golden stars down the leg: Adult Elvis Fancy Dress Costume, by George at Asda. £15.99. *Of course it was.*

The Indian man and his friends turned around and stared at him with incredulous faces. For the briefest of moments, Elvis fantasised that they thought he was the real King, as preposterous as he knew it was.

"Mate, your nose is bleeding."

"Yeah," said Elvis. His brain scrambled around. "I just… er, had a nosebleed."

"And one of your shoes is missing."

"Yeah, I… well, I lost my ... you know."

As if reading his mind, the Asian Elvis offered him a cigarette. "My name's Ravi, mate."

Elvis shook his hand and pushed his lips into something resembling a smile. He puffed ferociously on the cigarette. His bloodstream readily welcomed the nicotine and the relief.

"And your name is…?"

"Sorry, yeah. It's Elvis."

"Ha, good one!" Ravi said with an uncertain smirk. "You were really good man, *really* good. I mean I didn't know that second song, but you aced it. Way better than me."

Elvis wanted to say thank you, but he wanted more to scream. He did neither.

"You probably could do this for real, you know, like professionally," Ravi said.

"Yes, I've been told."

Ravi blew out thick white jets from his nostrils. "So, I saw you handing out flyers to some Elvis convention. You going?"

"I organise it." Elvis saw the man exchange furtive glances with his friends. "You interested?" he asked, unsure why.

Ravi guffawed. "A convention? No way man, that sounds totally…" His grin dropped. "I mean, no thanks, sorry. I'm not… that's probably more for like *proper* Elvis fans. To be honest, I just did this for a dare." Ravi's voice sounded distant and muffled, as if he was floating away. "My mate Jason here bet me fifty quid. Plus there's the hundred from winning. I didn't actually think…"

Elvis shut his eyes for a small eternity. He felt blood trickle down his chin.

"Hey, are you sure you don't need a tissue or something?"

With his eyes still closed, Elvis shook his head slowly, and Ravi stopped talking. For the briefest of seconds, he pretended this was a dream and he would wake up in his bed. He opened his eyes, and glanced over at Ravi and his friends like they were mosquitos, buzzing around his head. They gradually drifted away into their own conversation. He found himself humming 'I can't help falling in love', even though he didn't remember thinking about that particular song.

He looked down and saw drops of blood all over one shoe and one sock. The gold tassels were still in his hand. He marvelled at the thickness of the material. At least it felt authentic. He smiled. *Authentic*. The word resonated somewhere deep. In his bones. NOT a novelty.

He threw his head back and burst into song. In his peripheral vision, the pesky mosquitos drifted away. One of them guffawed. Another one shushed him. "TAKE MY HAND, TAKE MY WHOLE LIFE TOO. FOR I CAN'T HELP FALLING IN LOVE WITH YOOOOOOOOU," he bellowed, somewhere between singing and screaming.

How could he have known that song, those words, intimately for decades, have performed it on stage for perhaps fifteen years and only *now* just realise? Those words were for *him*.

Only for him. A phrase to sing to the King to show him how he truly felt. To emphasis his pure dedication. And he knew then. He *knew*, that the King had forgiven him. All was good.

18 Cut Strings *by Ander Louis*

Author's note: There are stories that have cropped up in all different societies independently throughout human history. They represent human realties using symbolism, and we call them myths. Cut Strings was my attempt to write something like a new myth that doesn't echo back throughout time, but in a new way feels symbolically human.

*

And then I was motoring across this dark lake, in the dark. I was peering forward into the darkness, determined to illuminate something monstrous, some horror lurking in the fog, something perpetually beyond the reach of my torch.

Then, through the fog there was a pier, vaguely, and a man.

"Funny old night," he said.

I coasted closer, then I was roping my little tinny to the cleat and disembarking onto his pier. The tinny pulled back against its tether, preferring the open water.

"What's that?" I asked.

"Funny old night," he repeated.

He was old – quite old – hunched on a stool, and between our words was silence, and a fishing rod was tucked below his stool with its line extended.

"Are you okay?" I asked. I hadn't expected to find anyone all the way out here.

"Oh yeah," he replied. "Never mind about me. You just keep exploring, keep on searchin'."

I made towards the land, saying "Thank you," with a nod, but the man said, "Young man, I know what you're looking for," and I stopped.

"I'm an explorer," I said. "I'm here to discover something new, that's all."

"Nah, nah, nah. That's not it."

"Okay," I agreed, and again I gave a nod, and ...

"Something old – that's what you're after. Ancient, prehistoric …"

A little less politely I nodded, saying, "Okay, sir. Have a good night then," and then I left the old man where he sat.

I could make out trees at the end of the pier, a thick, dark forest, and with a chill of anticipation I smiled gently. This was just what I lived for. Certainly there'd be something new in there. My pace quickened, the rickety boards beneath me creaked and groaned. I wasn't concerned about finding an easy path into the forest – the line of pines before me was now like an enemy front, and I: a hero-knight, charging into battle. I wanted to clash, tumble into the darkness. I wanted to do battle with the deep, dark unknown. Moonlit chaos in a forest!

I touched my pocket; pen and notebook accounted for. And then…

"Wrong way," he called.

His voice cracked through the silent fog and I paused like a prey animal.

"You don't wanna be goin' in there, you wanna be comin' back now."

I called back to him, "I'm not afraid," and he said, "Oh, I know that much. I'm saying – if you'll listen – that I know what you're lookin' for, young man! And I'm tellin' ya where it is – and it ain't that way. Understand?"

I turned my torch on him, he was looking out over the water.

"Come on, hear an old fella out. You're an explorer, aren't ya? Didn't you say that? You want something new?"

"New discoveries. I want to journal new discoveries and take them back to my university, to study…"

"Yes, yes, that. That's what I'm sayin', son, I'll tell ya

something new."

He was reminding me of visits to my grandma, and I sighed quietly as I recognised how impolite it would be to decline his offer. The forest would have to wait.

"It's not going to be something new though, is it?" I said, walking back along the pier. "Not if you're telling me it."

"It'll be new to you. Might be new to your university, too!"

"Right you are," I said. "What is it then?"

He nodded to the water. "In there," he said.

"What, in the lake?"

"Under it. Down the bottom. You'll definitely find something to take back to your professor down there."

"You're crazy if you think I'm going in there."

"And you'd be crazy to go in! Awful place. Dreadfully cold. Last place you'd wanna go."

"No kidding…"

"Dreadful place."

"Well… I thank you for the tip, but I'm going to…"

"That's where you'll find it, though. You'll always find the thing you want most in the place you least want to look. You'll always do that. Take it from an old fellow like me." He gestured to the water again. "Down there."

Timidly I peered into the water. It was black and still.

"Could I take the boat?"

"How do you suppose you'll take a boat to the bottom of a lake?"

Nervously I laughed. "Right… of course not," I said, and the black water remained black water, and transfixed on it now as I was, the moment became silent and long as the stubborn water refused to move. I peered harder still, and harder, and soon I found myself desperate for some horror to lurk up through the blackness and beckon me in, or to burst out and pull me under.

"Any tips?" I asked, and by now I was mesmerised – completely unable to wrench away my gaze from the water, scared though I might be.

"Yessss. Oh yes, yes, yes! Start here, young man: with the supposition that you, young man, might be special."

"I might be special…" I repeated dolefully.

"Yes, that's right! And your professors might be fools…"

Gently I swayed forward.

"Fools…"

"Your universities are made of string and driftwood."

"Is-dis-ooh –"

My thoughts were a cloak around a strider's ears, my words mere echolalia.

"And if you'll only see the strings, young man – see them!"

"See-see-see…"

Further I tilted forward, all I saw now was the black – the deep, dark black.

"You might understand you're not a puppet after all."

"Noh-noh…"

"But an anchor!"

"No!"

And then – I was in the water.

Awful place to be, cold and black. Immediately I felt I needed air and I strived towards the surface, my heart throbbing in my chest. Towards the surface… Up, and slowly up, a million miles up, until gasping I breached back into the night.

The old man peered down at me.

"Cold?" he asked.

"Cold," I squeaked, and then something brushed my ankle. And then it snaked around my ankle, then my calf, and then with a yank it wrenched me under.

I shook the tendrils away as they felt out my wrists and

feet and waist – but I was no match for these snakes, twisting their way around me from every angle. My feet were pulled together. I was screaming by now, uselessly screaming into the water. I felt my body bump against the bottom of the lake, and I was pinned to it by these crawling snakes. Like quicksand I sank into the mud until I was entombed, and then I fell through, out the other side, and entwined in snake-ropes I hung from the ceiling of an underground cavern, sopping, and I breathed in the stale, dead air.

The underworld. That's where I was, I felt that must be it, and I soon learned that the most frightening thing about the underworld is that there is no one else in the underworld. I heaved in the air, thin and acrid, and listened as the splashing of water echoed around me. I twisted in my constraints to no avail, I was bound too tight and there was no getting loose. It seemed that by now the snakes had hardened into vines of ivy, and I was part of this hanging tree.

I could see – I noticed with some alarm, and it was firelight that I could see by, the ivy leaf shadows dancing by the flickering of a small fire across the cavern.

A man stood, his shadow flew up the wall.

"Help!" I said. "Help me!"

There was a scream, a wailing, guttural scream, and I noticed behind him was a woman, naked and wide-eyed, sitting by the fire with her back against the wall. Cradled to her chest was an infant, and she curled it closer to her as if to hide it.

The man – or was it an ape? – leaned forward. Squinting he took one footstep closer, his hands were poised together at his chest, poised to block, or strike, or grab.

"Please," I whimpered.

Again the woman squealed. "Don't you dare," she was saying to the male – though without language – "You stay away from that thing."

He dismissed her with a grunt and crept closer. Below me I could see my things – my notebook, my torch, and my knife.

"Knife," I said, though I knew this creature did not speak my language, or perhaps speak language at all.

He was thinking, hard, I could see him listening, watching. He bent and picked up the knife, then with a grunt of surprise, he dropped it and recoiled. His partner cried out to him again from beside the fire.

"Please!" I urged, "Please, I won't hurt you. Just cut me down."

He turned away.

"Wait!" I urged, and he paused. She screamed. The baby remained silent. "Please…"

He turned back, looked at the knife below me. The woman stood and made to leave through the dark tunnel. She'd seen enough.

"Yes, the knife. Hand me the knife. Or cut me down."

He came closer – nose to nose – and he sniffed me, and I sniffed him back. He smelled of compost and fungi.

He bent, down, and came back up with my notebook. He thrust it into my hand and scampered away, grunting. The family left through the tunnel, and that was it from them.

With my hands bound together, and my body trapped in the vines, I knew that this was the end for me. Carefully I drew my pen from the book, and

TWO

I did what I had done often in times of terrible uncertainty. I wrote. My hands were numb, dripping, the joints in my fingers brittle. I scrawled, *The abyss… has taken hold of me*. I don't know why I did it. I breathed the cavern's crisp air through both nostrils, cooling my throat. *I always thought the abyss would be the final place for me, the conscious grave. But here I am, and now I know, it is more like restless sleep.* At once the ink began to drip. It was as though the dried letters gave up their form and longed for the pen once more. Black drops wept off the page, dripping away. I held my breath. A rain of black drops fell, I heard them bell into the puddles below, but their belling noise was not without light. One of the ripples glowed green. Then my words appeared in the ripples. Green letters in the black water. *Abyss. Conscious. Restless. Grave.* The letters spread apart like flotsam in a wild sea. More letters appeared, unbound by words. Soon the floor of the cavern was dressed in green words and abandoned letters, glowing like primeval mushrooms. I drew out my pen and wrote more, and as I wrote, the words could hardly keep to the page. They dripped off the paper and rippled through the cavern. I didn't mind, I thought I was hallucinating anyway. So I watched my words cascade onto the ground below.

The cavern glowed pearlescent green.

THREE

On the pier above, the old man felt his line go taut, and with a grunt of surprise, took the rod from under him and began to wrestle with something from the deep.

Something *big*.

"We got one," he said. "Here she comes!"

The pier rattled beneath him while he battled the fish for nearly an hour. It was slow work, but when a bite came, he was young again, such was the adrenaline that flowed through him.

Finally the thing surfaced. He heaved it up onto the pier. It was too gigantic and too exhausted to flap about, instead it just pulsed rhythmically. For a moment the old man kneeled beside the thing, catching his breath and steeling himself for the task at hand.

He began to prod along the fish's belly until he found the spot he sought, and there he slid in the blade of his knife.

"Sorry, ol' girl," he said.

She didn't seem too much to mind.

Carefully he towed it along. The slit seemed willing to grow, like a splitting pea. Inside, a lumpy cul-de-sac was intact, and he could see movement within it. He nicked it slightly, then the knife was put away and he pried the membrane open with his fingers.

"Ohhh," he sighed, "there you are!"

From inside the pulsing fish he extracted a tiny infant boy. His cry pierced the night. The old man wiped him dry, then wrapped him in a cloak.

"Shh-shh-shh, we'll get you home. It's too cold out here for a little bubba."

The baby was placed on the pier while the man shoved the fish back over the edge and gathered his things.

"Shh-shh-shh…"

The baby wailed into the night. He picked it up and headed off the pier, and into the forest.

"Shh-shh-shh," he soothed. And still the baby cried.

19 Fair Game *by Magz Morgan*

Author's note: This story contrasts the perspectives of young girls parented in very different ways, their coping strategies and how their relative positions change due to one pivotal event.

*

"Another child abducted. This time murdered. They found her in the woods. Been interfered with. And those others, one stuffed down a well and another in a cupboard. Awful. Imagine doing that to them," the paper rustled violently in their grandmother's hands.

"Hush, Mother! The children ..."

Linda the older girl, stared down at her food, frozen with shock. She didn't want to see her horror confirmed on the women's faces. It made her fears too real, too menacing. She darted glances at the other guests in the breakfast room of the BnB. Her little sister was intent on dragging toast soldiers around in the egg yolk on her plate.

On their arrival the day before, Buddy Holly's music ushered in the landlady's daughter grinning confidently from the doorway, a large gobstopper bulging in her cheek.

"Hello, I'm Sally," she'd said, rolling the candy around in her mouth. She had taken the group up to their rooms and set out the towels. The room with the single beds was for the two sisters. Their mother and grandmother were to occupy the other room.

Linda felt like a third wheel. She'd been forced to miss school to babysit her little sister while the two women attended to more important business. But she didn't dare voice that objection. Linda resented missing school. She'd surprised everyone by winning a scholarship. She missed the security of the routine, the days filled with quick-witted friends, with

120

books, words and creativity. Linda guessed Sally to be about twelve or thirteen as she herself was. Catching a glimpse of herself in the mirror, Linda flushed at her own sensible dress and the flat lace-up shoes her mother insisted on.

As Sally lounged in the doorway, her unruly black curls, tightfitting roll-up jeans and forthright manner unnerved her. The girl then did an about-face and thundered off down the stairs. Intrigued by this prospective new friend, Linda saw new possibilities in the seaside holiday her mother had promised.

Over the following days, a cold half-light filled their room and raindrops skimmed down the panes of the skylight. Linda was filled with dread at the prospect of the hours spent alone babysitting her boisterous younger sister. A small cupboard set into the back wall of their room gave her goose bumps and from time to time she jiggled the key to make sure it was locked. Every time the tree branches scratched on the attic windows she jumped.

For once in her life, she wished she were one of those carefree girls who lived for netball and rounders, girls who giggled and read movie magazines. She wished her head weren't swarming with Edgar Allan Poe, Alfred Hitchcock and Agatha Christie. Too many skeletons, cadavers and monsters from the grave inhabited the space behind that small door.

After a few days Sally appeared at the door whenever Linda's mother and grandmother went out. Sometimes the girls went downstairs to play in the breakfast room, hiding frantically when the landlady approached. Sally's games and ribald jokes at the expense of the adults always pushed the limits, were just out of view or hearing of the paying guests. Whenever Sally incurred a scolding, her eyes simply glazed over. Later, she said things to buck them up, telling them to pay no attention, that her mother's memory was rubbish. She sometimes said that her mother was full of hot air. Linda didn't know what that meant but she'd overheard her grandmother whisper to her mother, "The woman's a boozer. Common. Let's the girl skive off school." Linda didn't know anything about Sally's father. She'd never seen him.

One day their new playmate came to visit them up in their garret. Solemnly surveying the room, she pointed to the little cupboard recessed into the back wall.

"Bet you don't know what's in there," she said. Linda drew back in alarm, gruesome images seeping out. She reached out for her little sister and gripped her tightly. Sally laughed and lunged at the pair, "Boo!" she said, making them jump and the little one started to cry.

"It's nothing scary. Don't cry Rosie. Here have a lollipop," Sally said, handing it to the little girl who instantly stopped crying and made a grab for it.

"So, don't you want to have a look? I hid his magazines there under some towels when Dad left," said Sally. After that, Linda, feeling emboldened by Sally's matter-of-factness, sometimes pulled out some of the magazines and marvelled at them when her mother went out. Linda slid the magazines out, peeped at the pictures, snapping them shut at every approaching footstep in the hallway. She couldn't work out why any woman wanted to get undressed for a magazine, never mind bending over naked. And she couldn't work out why Sally's dad wanted to look at that.

One unexpectedly warm and sunny afternoon, Sally knocked on their door saying she had pocket money and asking if the girls could come down to the esplanade for some ice cream. To Linda's surprise, her mother agreed and gave her some pocket money too.

"Just this once, Linda. Nanna and I have an important appointment so it's handy actually. Now, all stay together and make sure you're back by five o'clock. Not a minute later. "

Half an hour later, the trio arrived at the esplanade and soon they were inside one of the games arcades, all flashing lights, pings, bells and juke-box music. Some local teenagers were lounging over the pinball machines and they greeted Sally with play-punches as she led her two new friends from machine to machine, periodically stopping to play. To the delight of little Rosie they won a few trinkets.

Before long, Linda realised that their games were being paid for by a man. An older man, a stranger. He had appeared from nowhere. Yet there he was standing close behind them, watching their games. She could feel his breath on her neck. He bent over and put his hand on her shoulder, gradually sliding it down her arm. Her first impulse was to run, to scream -- but every muscle, every nerve was frozen. She had no idea what he wanted but she knew this was odd, somehow wrong, very wrong. She wanted to run, to put distance between herself and this awful nameless feeling, this awful nameless man. Her mouth was dry and her tongue stuck fast. Shivering, she lowered her eyes, gripped her little sister's hand tightly and took a step away. His hand dropped but she had the memory of his body brushing up behind her. Had her friend noticed?

"Terrific game, girls! Let me pay for your next round," he said. Sally laughed, "Might as well," and let him pay for several games in a row. When she won more lollipops the smallest girl jumped with delight. Sally thought she had him worked out, whispering to Linda,"Silly old goat. He's always hanging around. Lives down our street somewhere." Then he suggested a ride on the big wheel, "What do you think of that?" he said.

"No thank you," Linda said and gripped her little sister even more tightly. That wasn't the arrangement. They were to stay together, as her mother had instructed them to do. She wanted to say something to Sally but she couldn't find the words.

"Oh well, if you don't want to come, what about you Sally?" he asked her.

"Why not? Just one ride. Wait for me, ok?" she called out to them. Watching her from the ground made Linda feel giddy and she began to tremble. The ride seemed to go on forever. Sally was waving wildly at them and the other two girls waved back. At the end of the ride, the man and the other girl didn't get off. Soon they were going round and around again. Little Rosie tugged vigorously on her sister's hand trying to pry herself loose. She'd had enough. As her older sister tightened her grip she started to cry loudly. Linda was rigid, her eyes scanning the big wheel for her friend who seemed to be lost to that ever-spinning machine. It was already past four o'clock and starting to drizzle. She felt her stomach churn.

Eventually, the giant wheel halted and Sally came flying towards them.

"Run! Run!" she said,"Don't stop." Her wild locks streamed behind her and there was something different about her. Gone was her usual confident demeanour. A sickening sense of dread crept over Linda's being. She felt her heart pounding, the blood pumping in her temples. Her legs carried her in and out of light and shadow as the trio flew down narrow laneways, through parkland and across busy roads.

"I think we lost him. The creep," Sally said. There was something diminished about her, she seemed somehow deflated, the colour drained from her face. Her normally steadfast gaze and toothy grin were replaced by downcast eyes and a tightness around her mouth.

"That sleazy pervert."

"Wha-a-a-t?" Linda gawked. Sally looked back at her then dropped her eyes. Linda could hear her breathing. Twice Sally opened her mouth to speak, hesitated then swallowed.

"Don't you get it, you idiot? Why didn't you go and get help?" By this time, Rosie was howling loudly. "Can't you make her shut up?"

"I – I – I thought you were just waving at us." By now, she wished the earth would open up and suck her down into a dark pit. She wished she were at home in bed hidden under the blankets and safely near her mother. A sense of the unfairness of it crept over her. She had followed her mother's instructions, eluded danger. Nevertheless, she had found herself being screamed at by someone she had trusted, someone she had considered a friend. Worst of all, she felt childish, immature and silly.

Then to her horror, Sally started wailing with rage. "Fuck the lot of you!" Linda stood there frozen to the spot, her little sister still howling. She waited for Sally to cry herself out in the dark. Then Sally looked at Linda, said sorry, said that she had nobody to tell, nobody would believe her and her mother was useless, she was sick of being the grown-up for two clueless parents.

The miserable trio walked the rest of the way home in silence. When they reached the BnB, Linda's mother yanked her elder daughter inside and slapped her face.

"It was my fault," Sally said in a low voice as the scene played out in front of her.

"How dare you disobey me? Do you know what time it is? Do you have any idea how worried we were?" Tense with fright and anger, she gripped her daughter by the shoulders. A sliver of silence hung between them. The colour returning to her face, their mother enfolded her two girls in a tight embrace.

Standing hunched against the door, Sally felt a dark stone within. A strangled look masked her face. From the depths of that mask, her eyes blinked rapidly. She felt betrayed by life. In the living room, her mother was deep into the bells and buzzers blaring from her favourite television game show.

20 Everyday Stranger *by Solène Anglaret*

Author's note: Unusually structured, disarmingly honest, and full of existential questions, 'Everyday stranger' is an ode to humanity that celebrates wholeheartedly both our differences and our similarities.

*

Growing up, Sunday mornings used to be my favourite. I would stretch in bed like a cat before running down the stairs to the kitchen. I can still remember waking to the smell of coffee and freshly baked bread, to the singing of birds in the garden and to the familiar and comforting sound of my parents' voices. Quickly securing a seat at the table, I would let out a cute little giggle as I reached for one of the warm and fluffy croissants. That was then.

A lot has happened.

A lot has changed.

A lot has been lost.

'Happy Sunday' I think to myself as I lay in bed determined not to move. It's past lunchtime already but I don't feel rested whatsoever. Why am I always so exhausted? Alone in my flat – somewhere in the heart of Shanghai's concrete jungle – it is to complete silence and emptiness that I open my eyes after yet another tormented night. I wonder when the vivid dreams and lifelike nightmares began. Perhaps they have always been there. Who knows? It seems like my brain is having a conversation with itself right now.

Will the nagging inner voice stop?

Will my brain ever quieten down?

Will I do something this Sunday?

As I attempt to stretch like I used to, my bones click loudly. Shoulder. Neck. Ankle. Knee. My dad, a lively wine connoisseur, often compares me to a piece of furniture without the screws. Listening to these painful clicks, I think he might have a point. Unlike good wine, time is not kind to our bodies but is it kind to our minds? There we go again. Wandering thoughts fill my brain which probably resembles an overflowing infinity pool right now. 'Focus', I mutter to myself as I stand up and get dressed. It is decided, I am going for a walk today. Why not?

Overwhelming heat.

Overwhelming beat.

Overwhelming leap.

As soon as I step into the city, the temperature and the humidity hit me. Like an invisible armour, a thick layer of sweat immediately covers my whole body. Hot and sticky, Shanghai summers make you feel as though you are stuck in a washing machine in the middle of a heavy rinse. I do not think I could ever become accustomed to this and it looks like most people agree. The streets are empty. The clouds are low. The air is heavy. One of the biggest cities in the world deserted. What am I doing out here again?

Left then right.

Step by step.

Here to there.

As I walk along the narrow streets of the Former French Concession and marvel at the architecture that surrounds me, I reflect on my recent trip back "home". Inverted commas. I can't help but use them. I've tried without. I really have. But I can't. I really can't. Why?

A party.

A story.

Let it be.

A week ago, I was in Paris having dinner with a few friends. They smiled when I arrived and we hugged when I left. That is the only warmth I felt. In between, no one asked about my life in China, my travels around Asia, my full-time job or anything else for that matter. They spoke about films I hadn't seen, music I hadn't heard of and memories I couldn't recall. There was a lot of drinking, talking and laughing. Not for me. I just left empty.

Distance too strong.

Been gone too long.

No longer belong.

There I was, a stranger in the place I am supposed to call home without inverted commas. A sudden outburst of sadness brings tears to the corners of my eyes. As I look for a tissue in my purse, I notice a cute little girl pointing her finger at me. She must be about six years old. "Lao wai, Lao wai, Lao wai" she screams at the top of her lungs with a defiant smile. My fingers linger into my purse and stumble upon my Alien Employment Licence. This little girl might be right after all. Foreigner, foreigner, foreigner.

This is who I am here.

This is who I am there.

This is who I am everywhere.

Or is it? Having spent more than ten years travelling and living around the world, I am starting to come to terms with idea that I do not belong anywhere. I looked long and hard for a place to call home but realised that home is more than just a place. It is also the people you surround yourself with. Those who love unconditionally. It is also yourself. The one thing you cannot go travelling without. Perhaps one does not need a place to have a home.

Foreigner.

Outsider.

Stranger.

I see the world differently. Some people say they think the globe is blue. Others say it is yellow or green. In my head, the globe is the most colourful painting I have ever seen. It is a canvas without borders and without structure. It is a masterpiece that is diverse, complex, and alive. Constantly evolving, it cannot be contained and is extremely difficult to describe. All the superlatives would not be enough to characterise its beauty and the diversity of those it is home to. Us. Despite our fights and misunderstandings, whether we like it or not, this is where we all live.

We are all human.

The world is one.

Tell everyone!

Can an everyday stranger bring us all together? As I turn a corner and greet the friends I am meeting for lunch, hope fills my heart and spreads through my veins. We are all from different parts of the world, different backgrounds, and different cultures. We might not speak the same mother tongue. We might not read the same books. We might not always agree on what food to order. Regardless, they know. They agree. They trust. This dream could become reality. Call me unrealistic or idealistic. Maybe utopian is who I am. Regardless, not an ounce of doubt in my body, a believer in a world without borders is who I choose to be.

Links to our world

www.worldwriterscollective.com

www.facebook.com/MelbWriters

www.meetup.com/Melbourne-Writers

www.meetup.com/All-Write